Skeleton Island

Skeleton Island

JAMES PATTINSON

ROBERT HALE · LONDON

© James Pattinson 1999
First published in Great Britain 1999

ISBN 0 7090 6470 5

Robert Hale Limited
Clerkenwell House
Clerkenwell Green
London EC1R 0HT

2 4 6 8 10 9 7 5 3 1

Typeset in North Wales by
Derek Doyle & Associates, Mold, Flintshire.
Printed in Great Britain by
St Edmundsbury Press, Bury St Edmunds, Suffolk.
Bound by WBC Book Manufacturers Limited, Bridgend.

Contents

1

Anchorage

THEY came to it early in the day when the sun was still no more than a glowing disc on the eastern rim of the sea. It was the kind of island on which in the bad old days pirates might have left buried treasure: small, tropical, roughly oval in shape, with a clump of palm-trees in the background and never a sign of any human habitation. On the chart it bore the name Dove.

'Nice,' Laurie said. 'Private. No crowds. That's what I like. Away from it all.'

There was a small bay, a few rocks sticking up from the water on the north side, a fringe of foam along the shoreline where the breakers were in miniature too, lazily tumbling on the sand as though at the very limit of their energy, exhausted from the crossing of the Atlantic and now at their last gasp.

'Who's for going ashore?' Rayburn asked. He looked at the girls. 'What do you say?'

'Sure,' Jo said. 'Why not?'

And Pippa said: 'What else are we here for?'

So it was settled.

Rayburn steered the yacht into the bay, and they dropped anchor and furled the sails. It was all so still, so silent. It was as if the island had been waiting for them and nobody else. It was, as Laurie had said, private.

It was the good life, this, Rayburn thought; a pity it would so shortly have to come to an end. But the money was running out and facts had to be faced. It had been fine while it lasted; so different from those recent years of war, shepherding convoys in the Atlantic and the Arctic. He and Angus had been young naval officers: R.N.V.R., the Wavy Navy, so called because of the zigzagging gold braid of rank on the sleeves. They had served in corvettes and later in a frigate, and when they had been discharged some time after the end of the war they decided to take a protracted holiday before confronting the inevitable necessity of working for a living. It would come to that eventually, but they saw no need to rush things. They were still young, and surely they had earned some relaxation.

Rayburn suggested to Laurie that this was so, and Laurie agreed wholeheartedly.

'We're free now. So let's make the most of our freedom while we have the chance. No need to put the nose to the grindstone straightaway. We've been through the mill, you and I. Dammit, we're lucky to be alive. Isn't that so?'

'It is so,' Rayburn said. And it was no exaggeration. There were plenty of others who had not been so lucky; plenty who were now in Davy Jones's Locker, which was not a pleasant place to be. At least they had avoided that and might as well make the most of their good fortune.

Laurie was of Scottish descent, though he had in fact been born in London, where his father was a surgeon of some repute. It was his wish that his son should take up the same profession, and he was none too pleased when Angus refused to entertain the idea. As he told Rayburn, he had no desire to become a sawbones; indeed had an aversion to anything of the sort. And so he had told the old man.

'He couldn't understand it. Thought it was very perverse of me. Tried every kind of pressure; even said it was a noble profession and I ought to be proud to take it up. But I stuck to my guns, and in the end he had to accept the fact that a son of his was not irresistibly drawn to the prospect of cutting people open and fiddling about with what was revealed inside.'

Laurie was black-haired, tall and gangling, rather craggy of feature and somewhat long in the nose. He was quite unlike Rayburn, who was shorter and more solidly built, with fair hair and a more rounded face. Neither of them had the kind of classical good looks that might have made fortunes for them on stage or screen, but since they had no ambitions in that line it was of no consequence and did not bother them.

Stephen Rayburn's father was a successful operator in the City with fingers in a number of pies from which he was adept at extracting the juiciest of plums.

'He's loaded,' Rayburn had confided to Laurie. 'Absolutely stinking.'

And it was then that the idea came to him.

'Why don't you and I put the bite on our respective and respected parents for a dollop of the necessary to buy a boat and go in for a bit of cruising? Be nice to potter around the world – or at least part of it. What do you think?'

Laurie was all for it. 'We could play the returning war hero card. Done our bit for King and Country, not to mention the loving parents. Deserve something in return and all that sort of bunk.'

'Moral blackmail?'

'Of course. It might work.'

And in the end it had worked, though not without some stout resistance. But eventually the resistance was broken down and both parents coughed up quite generously. The only stipulation was that when the young men had finished their cruising they should both return to England and settle down to some steady employment. There could be no question of extra cash being advanced when the initial sum became exhausted; it was to be strictly a one-off arrangement. In this matter the eminent surgeon and the rich financier had conferred with each other and had come to an agreement. Neither was at all happy with the plan, but both felt that they did indeed owe something to the young men who had given so much of themselves in those past six years of war.

'My wife thinks we should do what they ask,' the surgeon said.

'Mine too.'

It was possibly the female influence that had finally tipped the scale in the returning heroes' favour.

The financier drank some whisky, fiddled with his cigar and said: 'Probably get themselves into trouble.'

'Very likely.'

'Nothing we can do about that, though. They're not boys.'

'Not any longer, no.'

'So it's settled then?'

'I suppose so.'

It remained to agree on a figure. Neither man liked to appear mean to the other, and the figure turned out to be quite a large one. Much to the delight of the sons.

They found what they were looking for in a boatyard in Gosport. It was not new; indeed it had been knocking around for a good many years and had taken part in the evacuation from Dunkirk. At least, so the boatbuilder assured them, though he might have been spinning a yarn to increase their interest. But it might have been true; all sorts of craft, almost anything capable of making the trip across the Channel, had taken part in that operation. So why not this one?

The name of the yacht was *Wanderer*, which seemed appropriate. It had had a complete overhaul and they were assured that it was in first rate condition and fully seaworthy. It had two masts and was ketch rigged and was fully equipped for cruising. There was an auxiliary engine for use when required.

They had a trial sail in it and found it handled well, and they had no doubt that this was exactly what they wanted. They paid in cash and the yacht was theirs.

They took leave of England and for almost a year they cruised in the Mediterranean, that sea which had so recently been the scene of much naval warfare. It was a great life; they could go where they wished: the Riviera, Italy, Greece, the islands beloved of Homer, Cyprus . . .

Tiring of this, they passed again through the Straits of Gibraltar and headed south to Madeira. From there they made the long haul to the West Indies, the trade winds blowing steadily for much of the way. There had been incidents of course; no crossing of the Atlantic in a small yacht was likely to be plain sailing all the way. But *Wanderer* had proved equal to every demand made on her, and they had no complaint to make in that respect; she was a fine craft.

They spent some time cruising from island to island in the Caribbean, meeting other sea gipsies like themselves who were living the itinerant life in small sailing-boats; letting the world go by and seldom bothering to catch up on the news of what was happening on the other side of the Atlantic. For the present events in Europe were too far away for them to feel involved.

Eventually they found themselves working their way along the coast of Florida and going ashore here and there to that popular playground of the rich, the retired and the just plain idle. Not that they themselves fitted any of these descriptions; they were neither rich nor retired, and though they were for the present engaged in no profitable work, they were certainly not idle; the handling of the boat made sure of that!

It was on a beach a few miles north of Fort Lauderdale, at a place called Longville, that they fell in with Pippa and Jo. The girls were sunning themselves in the kind of bikinis that revealed just what splendid bodies they possessed. It was an arguable question whether they picked up the girls or were picked up by them. It was of no consequence which it was anyway, since the result was the same; and agreeable to all concerned.

It did not take long to discover that these desirable young females were free of any attachments in the shape of husbands or regular boyfriends. It also appeared that they were not working girls there on holiday. In fact it seemed that their time was their own, and when it was suggested that they might like to take a cruise in the yacht from which the two men had come ashore they were not slow to take up the offer. And they seemed impressed.

'You have a yacht!' Pippa said. 'My!'

Rayburn guessed that she had in mind something rather more glamorous than *Wanderer*, but he saw no reason to disillusion her.

'Yes, we have. Why don't you come along and take a look at her?'

'Sure, why not?'

So they put a bit more clothing on and went along.

Longville did not boast anything that could be called a marina, but there was a jetty with a few boats lying alongside it. One of these was *Wanderer*, as Rayburn pointed out.

'You mean that's it?' Jo said.

'That's it.'

'And you call that a yacht?' Pippa said.

She sounded incredulous, and Rayburn had to admit to himself that she and Jo had some excuse for feeling a certain disappointment. In their minds they had perhaps been picturing some big motor yacht, gleaming with white paint and varnish and polished brass; the kind in which millionaires did their cruising. He feared that now they had seen what the reality was they would take a quick step back from the very idea of even having a closer look at such a boat.

But he was wrong.

'Why don't we all go aboard and take a dekko at the accommodation?' Laurie suggested.

So they did. They stepped down into the cockpit and went down the companionway to the saloon, which was something completely novel in the girls' experience and quite a wonder to them.

'You live in here?' Jo said. 'You actually live in here?'

'Some of the time,' Laurie said. 'There's a galley and a for'ard cabin too. Nothing palatial, but big enough.'

They wanted to see these too.

'What do you think of it all?' Rayburn said.

It was Pippa who answered. 'I think it's just cute.'

It was hardly the word he would have used, but he let it pass. At least neither of the visitors was recoiling in horror from the squalor of it all. Which was a good sign. Maybe they were not so unused to a bit of rough living, even if they did look like a million dollars. And when he suggested they should take a short trip out to sea and back again they accepted without hesitation.

So they took the trip and enjoyed it. It was a new experience for them and they liked the novelty. Maybe they liked the company too. Rayburn hoped so.

*

For the next few days the four of them were together most of the time. They had paired off: Rayburn with Pippa and Laurie with Jo. Pippa was the smaller of the two, and Rayburn found himself greatly attracted to her. Her full name was Pippa Hagan and he thought it suited her. She had jet-black hair cut in an urchin style, and there was a puckish look about her, with those lustrous wide-set eyes matching the hair in colour.

Jo van Fleet was taller; a honey blonde. The surname indicated that at least some of her forebears had been Dutch; maybe way back when New York was still New Amsterdam.

It was Laurie who suggested they should all go on a cruise in the yacht. 'Maybe down to the Bahamas. You ever been there?'

Jo said they had not.

'So now's your chance. What do you say? Won't cost you a thing. And you'll love it. Take my word.'

It took them very little time to think about it and decide to accept the offer. They went off to collect their gear, and about two hours later they were back with it. Not that it amounted to much: a couple of duffel bags and some toiletry and what they stood up in.

'So here we are,' Jo said. 'And I guess we need our brains seeing to, because we sure as hell must be plumb crazy to be doing this.'

'You'll never regret it,' Rayburn said. 'You're going to have the time of your life.'

'Well,' she said, 'you just could be right at that. One thing's for sure: it's gonna be a change. But whether it'll be a change for the better remains to be seen.'

'Oh,' Rayburn said, 'you can count on that. Satisfaction is guaranteed.'

Later he was to learn that there were very strong reasons for not refusing the offer that had been made to them. They were just about on their uppers; no cash in the kitty and owing rent on the apartment they were living in. They had escaped without paying the arrears, but were not troubled by any feelings of guilt for having done so.

'It was as crummy as they come,' Jo said. 'And believe you me they do come crummy in some parts. I never want to go back to a shithole like that.'

Pippa seconded that. 'Nor me neither.'

Rayburn grinned. 'So this is next best thing to a shithole. Is that it?'

They both laughed, but left the question unanswered.

By this time he and Laurie had come to the conclusion that they had taken on board a couple of female beach-bums who had been living by their wits and their undoubted physical assets. They might not have been out-and-out hookers; Rayburn felt pretty sure they were not; but perhaps they were not so very many steps removed. Not that he and Laurie gave a damn what they were; they just loved having them aboard. They gave an added zest to life.

The girls themselves had never been on a long sea voyage before, so it was a new experience for them. But they took to it with no trouble at all. They were not even seasick. Rather to Rayburn's and Laurie's surprise they turned out to be pretty handy in the galley and willingly took over the cooking and other chores. So what with one thing and another they were really earning their keep.

They cruised on a meandering southerly course, island-hopping, and the girls seemed to be enjoying it all the way. They had no idea that the money was running out, because this rather unpleasant fact had not been revealed to them. It might come as a nasty shock to them when they learnt that they would soon have to be dumped back in Florida when *Wanderer* and her crew set sail for England. Of course they must have realized that the present happy state of affairs could not go on forever, but maybe they just did not think about the future, content to take each day as it came and extracting all the pleasure they could from the present.

So they came to the island; one of the hundreds in the Bahamian archipelago that were uninhabited. From it no other land was in sight except for a coral reef not far to the north. A line of white foam could be seen where small waves broke on the reef, and a flock of seabirds had gathered as if for a conference.

There was so little sound now that the yacht had come to rest; just the faint rustle of the surf and the distant cries of the birds. Their own voices were like an intrusion, and the shadows of the masts lay motionless on the surface of the water.

'So what are we waiting for?' Jo said. 'Let's go.'

2

Discovery

THEY rowed ashore in the dinghy, which was kept when not in use lashed on deck, bottom up. It was such a small boat that there was scarcely room for the four of them in it, and they weighted it down so that there was little free-board. Laurie handled the oars, grunting with each stroke and beginning to sweat a little by the time they reached the shore.

They were all barefooted, the girls wearing shorts and T-shirts, the men in shorts only. When the stem grounded they stepped out into the shallow water and hauled the dinghy up on to the sand.

'What a gorgeous place,' Pippa said. 'Why doesn't anyone live here?'

Rayburn gave a laugh. 'What would they live on? Fresh air? Plenty of that. But it's not big enough even to develop for the tourist trade.'

'So it's just left here for people like us.'

'That's about it.'

'Lucky us.'

'Oh, sure,' Laurie said. 'We're the lucky ones. Free to come and go as we wish and not a care in the world.'

Which was not quite true, Rayburn thought. Because there was still that little problem of the money supply to worry about; and Angus knew that as well as he. Only the womenfolk were ignorant as yet of the worsening financial situation.

They did some exploring for a start. Not that there was much to explore. The little clump of trees and undergrowth that formed a background to the scene did not amount to much, and apart from the rocks at the northern edge of the bay there were no geological features worthy of note.

The day was really heating up now, and they decided to take a swim in the bay. So they stripped off what little clothing they were wearing and went in naked. They were all good swimmers and they frolicked around in the warm limpid water for quite a while before emerging to bask on the sand like so many human seals.

'Just think,' Jo said, 'of all those poor devils sitting at desks in stuffy offices or on the production lines in noisy factories. There they are slaving away for the meal ticket, while we're sunning ourselves on our own private beach. Aren't we the lucky ones?'

'You bet your sweet life we are,' Laurie said.

He stretched out a hand to caress her body with its overall golden tan and gave no hint of what he knew only too well, that this paradisaical existence in which they were for the present luxuriating was all too rapidly racing to its conclusion. He could have told her that soon these idyllic pleasures must be no more than a memory, and she herself, this adorable girl lying there beside him would have slipped out of his life as though she had never existed.

But he did not. It pained him to think about it; he wanted to keep her with him always, never to lose her. And he was pretty certain that Stephen felt the same way about Pippa. It had never been their intention to become so emotionally involved with the girls, but intentions went by the board when the inescapable fact was that Jo and Pippa were like the answer to a dream. They had both fallen in love; that was the truth of the matter. And this in itself was crazy; for what future could there be in it? What possible future at all?

'Suddenly, Angus,' she said, 'you've gone all quiet and thoughtful. What's on your mind?'

'Nothing of importance,' he said. 'Nothing that would be at all interesting to you, my sweet.'

Which was really very far from the truth; for why would she not be interested in something that concerned her so greatly?

When they had sunned themselves for a while they got the beach ball out of the boat and played around with it like kids in a fun park. It was when this game was in full swing that the whole aspect of the run ashore was altered, and the laughter and the horseplay ceased.

Jo was chasing the ball, which had been thrown towards the belt of palms and other growth, and as she was running towards it she suddenly gave a cry of pain and started hopping around on one foot.

The others gathered round and asked what the trouble was. She seemed to be making quite a fuss over something.

'I stubbed my toe against that damned rock,' she said, pointing at what appeared to be the top of a large stone just showing above the sand. 'Feels like it broke a bone.' She sat down and gingerly fingered the big toe on her right foot, wincing as she did so.

Rayburn walked over to the offending stone and shifted some of the sand away from it with his own foot.

'Well now,' he said. 'This really is interesting. Looks like we're not the first to have been here. Looks too as if someone got so attached to the place he decided to stay on. Though I'd make a guess he didn't have much say in the matter.'

The others, with the exception of Jo who was still nursing her damaged toe, went over to take a look for themselves.

'What are you babbling about?' Laurie asked.

'About a stone that seems not to be a stone at all. Looks to me more like a human skull we have here.'

He kneeled down and scraped more of the sand away with his hand. 'Yes, just as I thought. Alas, poor Yorick, I knew him well. Though of course actually I didn't. This fellow's a perfect stranger. Always supposing it is a he and not a she.'

Now that he had made this clearance the eye sockets and jaw of the skull were revealed, where before only the bulge of the fore-head had been above the sand. It was this against which Jo had stubbed her toe.

'Ugh!' Pippa said. 'How horrible!'

The two men were less affected by the gruesomeness of the discovery. They were simply interested in the mystery of how it came to be there.

'So,' Laurie said, 'our desert island wasn't entirely uninhabited after all. I wonder who this joker is and who buried him.'

'One thing's for certain,' Rayburn said. 'He's not going to tell us.'

'Do you think the rest of him is under there?'

'One way of finding out.'

Pippa had moved back from the grinning skull. She shivered, as though sensing a chill even in the hot sunshine. 'Surely you're not going to dig that thing up.'

'Why not?' Laurie said. 'He won't raise any objection. Pity we haven't got a spade.'

'We could use the oars,' Rayburn suggested.

'That's an idea.'

'I'll fetch them then.'

He ran down to the boat and was back very quickly, eager to start on the exhumation which neither of the girls was very happy about.

He handed one of the oars to Laurie and they set to work. Though not as good as spades, the oars served passably well in the rather soft sand. Soon it became apparent that the skull was attached to a skeleton. It had been revealed first because, so it seemed, the neck had been bent during burial, perhaps because the grave had not been quite long enough to accommodate the body at full stretch.

Jo and Pippa, overcoming their aversion, peeped into the grave. They had retrieved their shorts and T-shirts and put them on, as if in an access of modesty they felt reluctant to appear naked in the presence of this bony stranger. The men too had donned their shorts and were sweating from the labour of digging.

'Well now,' Laurie said, 'do we lift him out or leave him there?'

'Oh, don't touch him,' Pippa said. 'Cover him up again.'

Rayburn told her not to be so squeamish. 'He won't mind. Probably enjoy the fresh air. Can't you see how he's grinning? Good set of teeth too.'

'How can you talk like that?'

She turned away, and she and Jo stood well back from the grave while the men bent down and lifted the skeleton from its resting place. When they had laid it on the ground they examined it more closely.

'Something odd about this,' Rayburn said.

'How d'you mean?'

'Well, how long do you think he's been in there?'

'I don't know. I'm no expert.'

'Neither am I. But wouldn't you think there'd be some shreds of clothing left?'

'Things rot. Like the flesh.'

'In dry sand? And how about shoes? How about buttons, belt-buckles and so on? There's nothing.'

'So maybe he was stripped naked when they buried him.'

'Maybe. And maybe it wasn't so very long ago either. This is a very shallow grave. Get a strong wind and the sand might be blown away. Gulls or some such would take a feed, soon strip the bones clean.'

'But they were covered before we dug them out.'

'Another high wind could have blown more sand over them. It's all guessing anyway. We don't know anything for sure. We don't know how long he's been here or how long it takes for flesh to rot away in these conditions.'

Jo chipped in then: 'Suppose it's really really old. Like a pirate or something.'

'Could be at that,' Laurie said.

Rayburn had been prodding in the excavation with an oar. The blade went in only a few inches before coming up against something hard.

'That's strange.'

'What is?' Laurie asked.

Rayburn prodded again, at a different place, with the same result. 'This grave's got a solid bottom.'

'Rock?'

'Possible, but unlikely, I'd say.'

He did some scraping with the blade of the oar. When he had shifted the sand aside a flat surface was revealed.

'Aha! What have we here?'

Laurie had a look. 'Seems like a piece of wood. A board?'

'Or a box.'

'Could be.'

'And boxes don't get buried in the ground just for fun. Especially under the dead body of a man. This could be interesting. I think we should take a look at it. Lend me a hand.'

Between them they shifted more sand and disclosed a rectangular box about a foot long. It seemed to be wedged in with other boxes, and they had to get down into the grave to ease it free and lift it out by the handles at each end, For its size it was remarkably heavy.

In appearance there was nothing odd about it. It was just a plain unpainted wooden box, stoutly made and with the lid nailed down; the heads of the nails rusty and staining the wood around them. The only mark on the lid was an emblem of some sort, probably applied with the aid of a stencil. It was in black paint, but this had faded so badly that it was hardly distinguishable. However, on closer examination there could be no doubt what it was.

It was a swastika.

3

Discussion

'Now this really is curious,' Rayburn said. 'A box marked with a swastika buried beneath a skeleton on an uninhabited island. What are we to make of that?'

'Ask me another,' Laurie said.

Pippa gave a shudder. 'It's spooky. Don't you think it is?'

Jo agreed. 'Real way out spooky.' She and Pippa were staying well away from the bones. They seemed to be unhappy about the whole business. It had taken all the fun out of their day. 'Maybe we should just pack up and leave. Go look for someplace else. Some place with no skinny residents like that guy there to give you the creeps.'

Rayburn stared at her in disbelief. 'Even before we've opened this box to see what's inside? Not a chance. Haven't you any curiosity?'

She gave a shrug but said nothing.

'Question is,' Laurie said, 'how do we open it? Looks like it could be a tough job. We'll need a tool of some sort. Can't do it with our bare hands.'

That much was obvious. But they had no tool with them. The need had not been foreseen when they came ashore. Laurie volunteered to go back to the yacht and fetch what was necessary.

'It won't take long.'

Rayburn accompanied him to where the dinghy was beached, carrying one of the oars. The girls came too; they seemed averse to staying with only the skeleton for company. Rayburn lent a hand to push the boat into the water, and Laurie got in and began to row. The others stood and watched him.

As he had said, it did not take long. Soon he was back, bringing with him a claw hammer and a cold chisel. Rayburn helped him beach the dinghy again, and then they all went back to where the skeleton and the box with the swastika mark were waiting for them.

Laurie set to work at once with the hammer and the cold chisel. He had to split the lid to get it off, but it was soon done. He ripped away the splintered wood and the contents were revealed.

Rayburn gasped. 'Oh my! Just take a look at that!'

Fitting snugly inside the box were two slabs of dull yellow metal. It was hardly necessary to examine the mark embossed on each of them to realize that what they had uncovered were ingots of pure gold.

'Would you believe it!' Laurie breathed. 'Would you bloody believe it! No wonder the box was so heavy.'

The girls were staring, wide-eyed. They were no longer thinking of the grim, silent watcher who had been the guardian of this treasure ever since it had been buried there.

'It can't be true,' Pippa murmured. 'It just can't be true. It's a dream. Soon we'll all wake up.'

Rayburn laughed. 'No dream, this. It's solid gold. Now aren't we the lucky ones!'

Laurie eased one of the ingots out of its nest with the aid of the chisel. He held it in both hands, feeling the weight of it.

'Now I'll tell you something. I never thought I'd ever be holding this much gold all in one piece. It's pretty heavy. Feel it.'

He handed the bar to Rayburn.

'Gimme, gimme,' Pippa said. 'I want to hold it.'

Rayburn passed it to her and she almost dropped it, taken by surprise at its weight. 'Oh, golly! It sure is heavy.'

'Still think it's just a dream?'

'A sweet dream if it is.'

'Even with old bony over there?'

'The skeleton at the feast,' Laurie said. 'Don't mind him.'

They were all feeling somewhat light-headed, like people who had backed a winning outsider at the races or hit the jackpot in a game of chance. For this really was some jackpot, since besides the ingots in the box they had taken from the hole there were other boxes still to come, and when they had uncovered and counted them all there were forty-nine of them. There could be little doubt that each of these boxes contained two more bars of this precious yellow metal that so many men had died for and killed for and worked like galley slaves to extract from a grudging earth.

But now there was much to think about. And gradually the euphoria passed and they began to consider all the questions that were begging to be answered. Questions like: Who had put the gold there, and why? And would they be coming back for it? And if so, when?

'One thing we can take for certain,' Rayburn said. 'Whoever they were, they meant to come back for it. Because nobody leaves a load of gold lying buried on an island just for the hell of it.'

'But it's been here a long time,' Laurie said. 'This character here tells us that. He didn't get to be the way he is overnight.'

Jo suggested that nobody ever was coming back for the treasure. She put forward her idea of pirates for consideration again, but Laurie put the damper on that.

'Pirates didn't pick up gold bullion nicely packed in wooden boxes. Their loot tended to be rather more mixed; jewels and plate and Spanish doubloons, that sort of thing; which they stowed in sea-chests. This stuff is a lot more recent. And there's the swastika too. Doesn't that tell us something?'

'Like what?'

'Well, it was the Nazi emblem, wasn't it?'

'So?'

'So it could have some connection with them.'

'What sort of connection?'

'I don't know. But there has to be some meaning to it.'

'Which we may never find.'

'Oh, what's it matter?' Pippa said. 'Thing is, we have a load of gold on our hands and we better decide what we're going to do about it. Isn't that so?'

It was Rayburn who suggested they should give themselves a bit of time to mull things over before coming to a decision.

'And meanwhile it might be best to fill the hole in.'

He glanced out to sea, as if fearing that already some other vessel could be heading that way and that their excavation might attract unwelcome attention.

The others seemed to catch his edginess. It might have been the kind of feeling you had when there was a fortune in precious metal lying at your feet; the feeling that somebody might snatch it away from you in the very moment when you were exulting in the possession of it.

'Don't you think,' Jo said, 'we might take just the one piece back to the yacht? I'd like to look at it some more; I surely would.'

They all agreed to that suggestion. They put the bits of lid back on the opened box and lowered it into the hole and shovelled sand on top of it. Then Laurie walked over to the rocks at the edge of the bay and knocked off a lump with the hammer. He brought it back and partly buried it to mark the cache. Meanwhile Rayburn had dragged the skeleton in among the trees and kicked some rubbish over it to leave it half concealed. This done, they took the ingot and rowed back to the yacht with it.

It was now well on into the afternoon and they had eaten nothing since breakfast. None of them had given a thought to food; there had been too much else to think about.

The bar of gold lay on the table in the saloon. Rayburn and Pippa sat on one side of it with Laurie and Jo on the other. Night had fallen and the saloon was illuminated by an oil-lamp hanging in gimbals.

'I suppose,' Rayburn said, 'there is one important question that needs to be answered first.'

'What's that?' Pippa asked.

'Is it legal for us to hang on to the gold?'

'What's the alternative?' Jo asked. 'Leave it here for somebody else to find?'

'We could inform the authorities in Nassau. This island comes under their jurisdiction, I imagine.'

'Are you suggesting we let those guys get their sticky little fingers on our gold? That's plumb crazy.'

'We might be entitled to some reward. Part of the value perhaps.'

'Me, I wouldn't take a chance on that. No, sir. What's a possible reward or part of the value worth in comparison with the whole caboodle which we have right here in our hands?'

Rayburn consulted Laurie. 'What do you say, Angus?'

Laurie gave some thought to the question before answering. Then: 'Well, look at it this way. What moral right do the Bahamas government have to this gold just because somebody left it lying around on one of their islands?'

'If it comes to that, what right have we?'

'Strictly speaking, maybe none. But we found it, didn't we?'

'And finders keepers. Is that it?'

'You bet,' Pippa said.

'How about the people who buried it?'

'Oh, them,' Laurie said. 'Well if you ask me it's odds on they had no right to it. Else why did they leave it here? And why did they kill a man?'

'Yes,' Pippa said, 'why did they do that? It's not the kind of thing your honest upright citizens do, is it? My guess is they're crooks and stole the loot. Besides which, they could be all dead now, like the guy they left behind to rot.'

Rayburn could see that this was a distinct possibility. It would explain why nobody had come back to dig up the buried treasure.

'You could be right,' he admitted. 'But whether they're alive or dead is neither here nor there. It makes our claim to the gold no more valid.'

'Now look,' Laurie said. 'Why don't we take a vote on it? Those who think we should report the find to Nassau raise their hands. Those who don't, keep them down.'

No hand went up. Rayburn had been acting as the Devil's advocate, but he had no more desire to let the treasure go than any of them. It had come at such an opportune moment, just when the cash was running out and the good life must come to an end. It had to be fate stepping in to rescue them, and it really would be stupid to spurn the good fortune.

Laurie grinned at him. 'So you were bluffing. You meant to hang on to the yellow stuff just like the rest of us.'

'There was no point in my voting the other way. It would have been three to one.'

'Oh, sure. That was the only reason. Now pull the other one.'

Pippa said: 'How much would a bar of gold like that be worth? In dollars.'

'I don't even know what it would be worth in pounds sterling,' Laurie said. 'But you can bet it's quite a packet.'

'How much would you think, then?'

'Several thousand dollars.'

'How many is several?'

'Your guess is as good as mine.'

'Give me yours.'

'Let's say ten thousand, then.'

'And we've got forty-nine boxes with two in each. That's how many bars?'

'Ninety-eight,' Jo said. She was good at figures.

'And at ten grand apiece?'

'Nine hundred and eighty thousand.'

'Oh my! That's nearly a million, isn't it?'

'Sure is.'

Pippa clapped her hands. 'Whoopee! We're rich. We're rolling in it.'

Laurie sounded a note of caution. 'Hold on. We don't know those figures are correct. I was just guessing. This bar could be worth a lot less than ten thousand.'

'But it could be more, couldn't it?'

'Yes, it could.'

'Much more?'

'Possibly.'

'Either way it's going to be a lot of dough, isn't it?'

'Oh, you can bet on that. Gold bars don't just grow on trees.'

Rayburn said: 'Before we start counting our chickens there's another thing we have to think about.'

'What's that?' Pippa asked.

'How do we dispose of the gold?'

'We sell it, don't we?'

'That may not be as easy as it sounds. You can't just wheel a load of gold bars into a bank and demand payment over the counter in cash.'

It put a check on the exuberance. Neither of the girls seemed to have given a thought to this question, though it was possible that Laurie had.

Pippa frowned. 'I don't see the problem. Wouldn't a bank buy it from us? It's the sort of business they do, isn't it?'

'So it may be, but not quite in that way. Now supposing we did walk in with this gold. Don't you think they'd be a bit curious as to how we came by it. Don't you think they'd be on the blower to the cops to see if there'd been a raid on Fort Knox or wherever?'

'None of their damn business.'

'I think they'd consider it very much their business. And next thing we'd have a bunch of law officers breathing down our necks and giving us a bit of interrogation. Which would be more than a little embarrassing, wouldn't you say?'

'So you don't think banks are on the programme?'

'No, I don't.'

'Who, then?'

'Now that's a question that's going to need a lot of careful consideration.'

4

Suggestion

NONE of them went to sleep very early. Rayburn slept fitfully and dreamed of skeletons and vast amounts of gold for which he had to dig and dig and dig. When he awoke from the last of these dreams he found that the girls were already up and about; and he guessed that they had been having a conference between themselves. It did not take much guesswork to come up with an answer to the question of what the conference had been about.

It was not, however, until they were all having breakfast that Pippa brought up the subject of the gold and the problem of how to dispose of it.

'Jo and I have put our heads together and we think we've come up with an idea.'

'Regarding what?' Laurie asked. Though he must have known.

'The gold of course. What else?'

'Yes indeed,' Rayburn said. 'What else is of paramount interest to any of us just now? I dreamed about the stuff.'

'Me too,' Laurie said. 'I dreamt the skeleton had come to life and was standing guard over it with a flaming sword.'

'Look,' Pippa said; and she sounded exasperated. 'We don't want to hear about your dreams, interesting though they may be. I guess we all had them. Do you or do you not want to know what this idea is that Jo and I had?'

'Of course we do,' Rayburn assured her. 'Say on.'

'Okay then. It's a possible way of selling the gold without involving a bank.'

'Go on.'

'Well, Jo and me, we know a guy who may be able to help us. Advise us anyway.'

'This guy has a name?'

'Sure he does. Roy Carlson.'

'And why do you think he might help us?'

'He's in finance.'

'Any particular kind of finance?'

'Oh, he has plenty irons in the fire, I guess. He really knows his way around.'

It sounded rather vague to Rayburn. Maybe a bit dodgy too.

'How do you come to know this Mr Carlson? Have you done business with him?'

'Not exactly.'

'Have you known him long?'

'Oh gosh, yes. He's a friend. Ask Jo.'

Rayburn looked at the blonde for confirmation.

'You have my word for that,' she said. 'A real nice guy.'

But she would say that, wouldn't she? he thought. She and Pippa had cooked up the plan between them and both were bound to be all in favour of it. He himself had a feeling that this Roy Carlson might be some kind of slick operator in the money market who possibly was not too concerned regarding the strict legality of his operations. But was that not just the type of person they would need to deal with? He would certainly expect his rake-off however nice a guy he was. And however good a friend of Jo and Pippa he was, he would be looking for some commission even if all he gave was advice. But that was fair enough. If he pointed out the way for them to market the gold he would have earned his fee. Always supposing he did not demand too much.

He glanced at Laurie. 'What do you think, Angus?'

'Well,' Laurie said, 'I suppose it would bear thinking about. There's no hurry to come to a decision. If we don't come up with any better plan, it might be worth a try.'

'You don't sound very enthusiastic,' Jo said. 'Neither of you.'

'No reason why we should be. We don't know your man Carlson. All we have is your word that he's a nice guy.'

'Don't you believe it?'

'Of course I do. He's probably been as nice as pie to you. Who wouldn't be? But it's not really enough, is it?'

Jo looked sulky. 'We were just trying to help. But of course if you can do better, go ahead.'

Rayburn spoke placatingly. 'Now don't be ratty. Of course we're glad of any help you can give us. But we don't have to rush into anything without thinking, do we? What I suggest is we take this one bar for a try-out and see how it goes.'

'Where do we take it?' Pippa asked.

'I'd say the obvious place is where we came from. It's the near-est likely market. There'd be no point in carting the stuff across the Atlantic.'

'Sounds reasonable to me,' Laurie said. 'What do the ladies say? Are you in agreement?'

'Of course,' Jo said. 'It's the obvious place. And if we're going to consult Roy—'

'Where does he hang out?' Rayburn asked.

'Fort Lauderdale. He's got an office there.'

'Then we may as well go back to Longville. It's a nice quiet place and Fort Lauderdale is within easy reach. That's if you're not afraid your former landlord might come on to you for the rent you owe him.'

They both laughed at that. It was a prospect they appeared to find somewhat less than daunting. Maybe it was not the first time they had made a quick flit. During the weeks spent aboard *Wanderer* they had revealed very little concerning their background, and neither Rayburn nor Laurie had pressed them for information on the subject. Perhaps it was better not to know too much.

For their part they had been less reticent. It was noticeable that their companions were more than a little impressed by the fact that they had served in the Royal Navy during the war, and they were not averse to playing this card for all it was worth. And anyway there was little need for any exaggeration when the reality had been enough. It had been no picnic, so why pretend it had been? Especially with this audience.

On one occasion Rayburn said: 'She loved me for the dangers I had passed, and I loved her that she did pity them.'

'Now what was that all about?' Pippa asked.

'Take no notice,' Laurie said. 'He's just showing how literate he is. It's from Shakespeare, *Othello*. The Moor is speaking of the reason why Desdemona fell for him. You see the connection?'

'Oh, Jiminy Cricket!' Pippa said. 'See what we have here, Jo? Not only battle-scarred heroes but a pair of regular eggheads to boot. Aren't we the lucky ones! Two for the price of one.'

Later she said: 'Did you mean that, Steve?'

'Mean what, Pip?'

'That about loving me.'

'Bet your life. And you?'

'Me? Oh sure, I love you like crazy.' She kissed him to prove it. It was a real loving kiss and no mistake. As if she truly meant every word of it.

But he wondered whether either of them was really telling the truth or whether it was just a game they were playing. He was damned if he knew.

Laurie said: 'You never guessed when you signed up for a sea trip with us that it would turn out this way, did you? If we hadn't come along you might still have been in that lousy apartment wondering where your next crust was coming from.'

'That's true,' Jo admitted. 'Sure was our lucky day.'

It occurred to Rayburn that there had been no discussion about how the windfall should be shared out; somehow it seemed to have been taken for granted that they and the girls should each have an equal slice of the cake. And perhaps this was fair enough, since it was Jo's big toe that had discovered the cache. Nevertheless, he would have been rather less than human if the thought had never entered his head that without Jo and Pippa taking half the prize his and Angus's share would have been twice as large. Were they not at least entitled to a somewhat larger slice, seeing that the yacht which had carried them all to the island was theirs, and that they had paid all expenses? Possibly. But having reflected in this way he thrust all such arguments aside as being mean and selfish in the extreme. The four of them were in this together and it had to be equal shares for all.

'Righto then,' he said. 'Since we've decided where we're going, we might as well be on our way.'

There was no argument about this. The gold was a great incentive to set things in motion.

5

Phone Call

IT was a distance of some two hundred and fifty miles. The winds were variable and the voyage took almost a week. They would have used the engine more, but they were short of petrol and had to conserve it. And then, when they were almost home, they were intercepted by a Coast Guard cutter.

It was a fine bright day, the sun shining, the sea calm, with only a light breeze ruffling the surface. As far as they were concerned there was only one thing spoiling the picture: this cutter flying the United States flag.

'Now this,' Laurie said, 'we could very well have done without.'

'Is it trouble?' Pippa asked. She sounded nervous.

'No reason why it should be,' Rayburn said. 'We're not breaking any laws.'

A voice floated across from the cutter, magnified by a loud hailer and ordering them to heave to.

'We are coming aboard.'

'It is trouble,' Pippa said. 'I just knew something would have to go wrong. We better hide the gold.'

'Now that would be the stupidest thing,' Rayburn told her. 'They'd be sure to find it and wonder why it was hidden. And anyway it's not what they're looking for; you can be sure of that.'

'So what are they looking for?'

'Contraband. My guess is drugs. Probably cocaine. We're clean, so there's no cause to panic. Just act natural.'

They lowered the sails and hove to. The cutter came alongside. It was a trim rakish craft which looked as if it might have a useful turn of speed if it had to do any chasing. The two men who stepped on board *Wanderer* were rugged-looking characters, deeply tanned and sure-footed. The one who appeared to be the senior introduced himself as Craig and the other as Landau.

'Where are you bound?' he asked.

Rayburn told him. 'Longville.'

'And where from?'

'The Bahamas. Just cruising.'

'For pleasure, huh?'

'That's it.'

'Nice,' Craig said.

He was glancing at the female half of the yacht's company and he might have been referring to them, but his face was expressionless. Landau also looked at the girls. He was younger than Craig and might have been wishing that he could afford to go cruising with such desirable companions. Jo smiled at him and he smiled right back at her, but said nothing, leaving it to the other man to do the talking.

Craig said he would like to examine the log, and Rayburn conducted him to the saloon, a corner of which served as a chart-room. There was a hinged table which was little more than a shelf, and above it were cubbyholes and a small bookcase. On the chart~table, amongst other things, was the gold ingot.

Craig saw it at once. 'What's that?'

'A paperweight,' Rayburn said.

It was in fact lying on some charts.

'Looks like a gold brick.'

Rayburn laughed. 'Wish it was. It'd be worth quite a few dollars, wouldn't it?'

'Guess so. But it's not?'

'Not a chance.'

He hoped Craig would not pick up the ingot. The weight of it might give him a suspicion that it really was gold, and then he might ask a lot more questions about it. Like why did they carry a lump of gold about with them and where did they get it? But really it was none of his business.

'You don't mind if we search the boat?' he asked, after glancing through the log.

'Would it make any difference if I said I did?'

Craig gave a wintry smile. 'Guess not.'

'Well, go ahead if you feel like it. You won't find any drugs, if that's what you're looking for. We're clean. We do our sailing strictly for the kick we get out of it. Smuggling's not our line at all.'

He was not sure whether Craig believed him. Maybe he had heard that tale before. They carried out the search anyway. It did not take long. Rayburn got the impression that they were just going through the motions and did not really expect to turn up any contraband. He thought of offering them some refreshment, and then thought better of it. They might take it as a bid to curry favour, and besides, why do anything to delay their departure?

As they were leaving Craig said: 'Have a nice day.'

'You too,' Rayburn said.

Jo watched the cutter speeding away and breathed a sigh of relief. 'Boy, am I glad to see the back of them! I thought that guy Craig was going to make something of the gold bar, He sure seemed interested in it.'

Rayburn told her she need not have worried. 'It wasn't what he was looking for. Now if we'd been carrying a batch of cocaine or heroin things would have been different.'

'There's a lot of it goes on, so I've heard,' Pippa said. 'Guys with boats go down to Colombia or some place where they can pick up a load of junk and run it ashore on the Florida coast. If they don't get caught.'

'It's sweet trade,' Jo said. 'I guess weight for weight coke is more valuable even than gold. You guys ever think of trying it?'

Laurie gave a laugh. 'You think we want to see the inside of an American jail?'

'Not everybody gets caught.'

'I wouldn't like to risk it.'

'There's big money in it.'

'So there may be. But just for the present I think we'll stick to buried treasure.'

'You've got no ambition,' Jo said.

Rayburn wondered whether it was just possible that she might not be kidding. There was a dreamy look in her eye, as though she had some picture in her mind, possibly of great wealth gained from the smuggling of heroin or cocaine into the eager market of the United States where the dollars were waiting. Somehow he doubted whether she would have been deterred by such a little thing as conscience. But perhaps he was misjudging her. He hoped so.

Wanderer slipped into the little harbour of Longville with no fuss and no ceremony. This was the kind of place where no large vessel ever came and no merchandise worth speaking of was handled. A few small offshore fishing-boats used it, and the odd travel-stained and unimpressive yacht like this one. Formalities on arrival were minimal, which suited Rayburn and Laurie very well. They berthed the yacht in much the same place from which it had departed not so long ago, and the retired ship's officer who laid claim to the rather grandiose title of harbourmaster came along to give them a look. He recognized them from their previous visit.

'So you're back again. Have a good trip?'

Rayburn said they had. 'It's been very pleasant.'

The harbourmaster, whose name was Jones, came aboard and did not refuse a glass of whisky. He was a weathered sort of man, grey-haired, bearded, walking with a slight limp. He was courteous to the girls in a fatherly kind of way, and Rayburn wondered just how much he knew about them and their mode of living. Perhaps a great deal; but if he did he was giving no hint of it.

Captain Jones, as he was known, asked no questions regarding the gold bar, for the simple reason that he did not see it. They had removed it from the chart-table and stowed it out of sight. It had seemed a prudent thing to do.

When the harbourmaster had left, the four still on board the yacht had a conference to decide what the next move should be. The time had come when the men had to make up their minds whether or not to fall in with the girls' suggestion of consulting the man named Roy Carlson.

'Well, are we or aren't we?' Jo demanded.

'You're sure we can trust him?' Rayburn asked.

'Would we ever have suggested going to him if we weren't? And anyway, have you thought of any better alternative? Other than walking into a bank and slapping the lump of gold down on the counter. Which I believe you yourself ruled out.'

Rayburn turned to Laurie. 'What do you say, Angus?'

'On the whole I suppose it's the best plan. After all, we'll only be risking the one bar.'

'What do you mean, risking it?' Jo said. 'You think Roy's the sort of guy who'd steal it from you?'

'I don't know what sort he is. I've only got your word to go by, haven't I?'

'And that's not good enough? So you don't trust me either? Well, now we know.'

She had become quite heated, and Laurie did his best to placate her. 'Of course I trust you, Jo darling. It's this Roy Carlson I'm not so sure about. Still, if you say he's okay, that's good enough for me.'

'So it's settled then?'

'If Steve's agreeable, I am.'

'All right,' Rayburn said. 'Let's give it a go.'

It was decided that Jo should get in touch with Carlson by telephone and arrange a meeting with him at his place in Fort Lauderdale. She was not to mention the gold but was only to say that they wished to discuss a financial matter of some importance.

'Do you think that will be enough to persuade him to see us?' Laurie asked.

'Oh, sure,' Jo said. 'You can depend on it. I know how to handle Roy.'

Rayburn thought she sounded very confident. He wondered just how close the relationship netween Carlson and the girls had been. But it was the kind of question it might have been less than wise to ask.

Jo went off to find a public telephone while the others waited on board the yacht. She was back very soon, looking pleased.

'So how did it go?' Rayburn asked.

'Like I said it would. Had him eating out of my hand. He'd like us to go over there straightaway.'

Rayburn was surprised. It was already well on into the afternoon.

'You didn't mention the gold?'

She gave him a withering look. 'I promised I wouldn't, didn't I? It just happens that I keep my word.'

He saw that she had taken offence again, and he hastened to

assure her that he was sure she did. 'I thought it might just have slipped out.'

'Well, it didn't. He doesn't have the least idea what it is we want to talk to him about.'

'I guess it'll be a surprise to him when he finds out,' Pippa said. 'I can't wait to see his face when we show him the gold.'

Rayburn just hoped they were doing the right thing. He had a feeling that he and Angus had been bulldozed into taking this step and that they might live to regret it. But the die was cast now and they had to go through with it.

6

Consultation

THEY travelled to Fort Lauderdale by bus. Jo was carrying the gold bar in a leather shoulder-bag which she had emptied of all the junk she usually carried in it. She remarked that the bag had never been so goddam heavy.

'Are you complaining?' Laurie asked.

'No,' she said. 'No complaints. Just an observation.'

It was a short journey along the coast and did not take long. It occurred to Rayburn that for a quartet who had almost within their grasp a fortune in gold bullion it was curious that they should be forced to make the journey in a racketing bus with a motley assortment of other passengers, including a number of noisy children. They ought to have been riding in a Rolls-Royce or at least a Cadillac. But the money was not in their pockets yet, and perhaps it was tempting fate to start making plans for the future based on a treasure that might yet slip through their fingers.

There were still a lot of scantily clad bodies laid out on the beach at Fort Lauderdale when they left the bus. There were other, more energetic bodies playing with beach balls or fooling around in the shallow water. Everywhere considerable quantities of naked suntanned human flesh was on display, much of which might have looked more attractive if it had been decently covered up.

But the beach was not the destination of the four seafarers. With the girls leading the way they moved away from the shore, Jo looking somewhat weighed down by the heavy bag hanging from her left shoulder.

It turned out that Roy Carlson had an office of sorts in a street quite some way removed from the seafront. It was in a rather old building, and on the heavy oak door was a brass plate which read: ROY A. CARLSON. FINANCE CONSULTANT.

'This is it?' Rayburn said. He was not very favourably impressed. It was not quite what he had expected; he had had something rather more modern in mind. But at least there was nothing flashy about this place of business. The stucco front was half covered with creeper of a kind he could not identify, and a wrought-iron balcony on the upper floor gave it a certain colonial look; French or Spanish perhaps. 'This is where our man hangs out?'

'Isn't that what it says on the door?' Jo said rather tartly. 'You can read, I suppose.'

'But this looks more like a private house than an office.'

'Well, he lives here too.'

There was a bell-push at the side of the door. She pressed it and they waited. But not for long. The door opened with so little delay that it seemed the man who opened it might well have been standing in the hallway in expectation of their imminent arrival.

'Hi, Roy!' Jo said. 'Here we are. This is Steve Rayburn and that's Angus Laurie. Pippa, of course, you know.'

'Sure do,' Carlson said. 'Mr Rayburn, Mr Laurie, very pleased to make your acquaintance.' He offered his hand to each of them in turn, and his clasp was firm. 'Don't get many English clients. Makes a change.'

'I'm Scots,' Laurie said. 'At least by parentage.'

'Is that a fact! There is a difference, I guess.'

Carlson was lean and rather above average height. Rayburn immediately classified him mentally as a handsome devil, maybe not altogether to be trusted. He was rather like one of those stars of the inter-war films: slick black hair that looked as though it might have been brushed with boot polish, smooth cheeks lightly tanned, small moustache, perfect teeth and a clean-cut chin. He was probably in his mid-thirties, or perhaps a well preserved forty.

He invited them inside and led the way to what was apparently the room where he conducted his business. It was equipped as an office, but there were enough chairs for all of them to be seated. Carlson positioned himself behind a large mahogany desk facing the others. He rested his elbows on the desk, made an arch with his fingers and said:

'Now what's it all about?'

'We could use some advice,' Rayburn said.

'So I understand. But with regard to what, precisely?'

'It's a question of selling something. Finding a market for it.'

'I see. And this something is what precisely?'

Rayburn hesitated, conscious of the niggling feeling of distrust in his mind. But having come this far, it would be absurd to draw back now. Besides which, it was not his decision to make. They had discussed the matter and had come to an agreement. So he turned to Jo.

'Show him.'

She stood up, carried the shoulder-bag to the desk, opened it and took out the bar of gold. This she laid on the desk for Carlson to see.

'There!'

Rayburn had expected him to react with some expression of surprise, but he did not. It was almost as though it had been the commonest thing in the world for clients to produce bars of gold from their handbags and lay them on his desk. So maybe he had known what was coming. Maybe Jo, despite her denial, had in fact told him on the telephone what it was they wished to consult him about. But really it made no difference. It was all one in the end.

'Now that,' Carlson said, 'looks to me very much like a lump of the yellow metal we all long to get our hands on. Are you going to tell me where you got it?'

'For the present,' Rayburn said, 'no.'

'Fair enough.' If Carlson was disappointed he hid the feeling very well. 'So this is what you have to sell?'

'It is.'

'And is this the full extent of the merchandise or is there more where this came from?'

'There's more.'

'Much more?'

'Enough.'

'But for the present you're not willing to tell me the exact amount of that either?'

'It doesn't seem necessary.'

'Perhaps not,' Carlson said. 'But tell me, do you have any idea what this bar is worth?'

Rayburn made no immediate answer, and Pippa chipped in.

'Ten thousand dollars.'

Carlson smiled. He lifted the bar in both hands, as if judging the weight of it. Then he put it down again.

'You're optimistic.'

'So what figure would you put on it?'

'Less than half that.'

Pippa looked disappointed. 'But that's just a guess too, isn't it?'

'True,' Carlson said. 'But I've had some experience with this sort of thing and I'd say none of you has. Correct?'

'Correct,' Rayburn said. 'That's why we're here. To get some advice.'

'Now let me make another guess. You thought about taking it to a bank, but decided that was not a good plan.'

They all stared at him but said nothing.

'You were right,' Carlson said. 'It wouldn't have been a good plan. Banks like to know who they're dealing with. They demand credentials. They ask awkward questions concerning the origin of the mechandise and how you came by it. You've thought of all that hassle and you've ruled banks out, haven't you?'

They remained silent.

'Yes,' he said, 'I see you have. So no banks. So you have to find an alternative market. Okay then, let's take it from there. I can find you a buyer.'

'You can?' Rayburn said.

'Oh, sure. But I have to warn you he won't pay the kind of price quoted on the bullion market.'

'Why not?' Pippa asked.

'The reason's obvious. He's not in the business for fun. He's got to make his profit.'

Rayburn said cautiously: 'This man you're talking about. What kind of price would he be likely to pay?'

Carlson pursed his lips. 'I wouldn't really like to hazard a guess. But it'd be as much as you could expect to get anywhere else with no questions asked.'

Rayburn had a suspicion that Carlson was talking about a crook; and if he had dealings with crooks it must surely mean that he himself was in some degree bent. Which just went to confirm that initial impression he had had of him. Again he felt reluctant to do business with such a man. But if banks were ruled out, where else could they go in their search for a gold buyer?

'You would be willing to introduce us to this trader?'

'If you wish. Naturally, I'd have to charge a fee for this service.'

'And how much would that be?'

'A commission of twenty per cent of the amount paid by the purchaser.'

'That's a bit steep, isn't it?'

'I wouldn't say so. Not for the kind of service I'm giving. Still, if you don't like the terms you don't have to take the service. The choice is yours.'

Rayburn appealed to the others. 'What do you say?'

Laurie said: 'Does seem a lot, but—' He gave a shrug.

'Oh, hell!' Pippa said. 'We can't go hawking the stuff all round the town. And I guess maybe we wouldn't get better terms anyplace else. So I say let Roy have his twenty per cent.'

Jo agreed with that. 'But you better deliver the goods, Roy. You better get us a decent price.'

Carlson gave a sly grin. 'You can count on it I'll do my darnedest. Why wouldn't I? The more you get, the more I get. Isn't that so?'

'How soon can you get things moving?' Rayburn asked.

'So you're going to let me do the deal?'

'Looks like it.'

'You won't regret it. Tell you what I'll do. I'll get in touch with the buyer and arrange a meeting for tomorrow. How does that sound to you?'

'Does this buyer live in Fort Lauderdale?'

'No. He has a place some way out of town. No problem. I can take you there in my car. All of you if you want to come along. I understand you have a boat over at Longville.'

'That's so,' Rayburn said. 'A small yacht. *Wanderer.*'

'Then suppose I pick you up at ten o'clock in the morning. That suit you?'

There were no objections. Now that they had decided to employ Carlson as agent there was no point in delaying things. Rayburn still had misgivings, but maybe it would all turn out fine in the end. He hoped so.

'You can leave this here,' Carlson said. He tapped the gold bar with his forefinger. 'I'll put it in my safe for the night.'

'No,' Rayburn said. 'We'll take it with us.'

Carlson laughed. 'Still not trusting me? Well, have it your own way.'

As they were about to leave Rayburn said: 'Incidentally, what's the buyer's name?'

'His name,' Carlson said, 'is Willem Blok. He's generally known around and about as the Dutchman, though you have my word he's as American as apple pie and cheese.'

'Suppose he doesn't want to trade. What then?'

'Oh, he'll trade when he learns there's more gold where this came from. He surely will.'

7

The Dutchman

CARLSON arrived dead on time. His car was a big Buick convertible with white tyres. He parked it at the head of the jetty, where it stood in all its glory of gleaming chromium plate and bright red enamel.

They were all in the saloon of the yacht, and he had stepped on board before they realized he was there. They heard the sound of his footsteps, and then he was looking in on them.

'So,' he said, 'this is where you live. Kinda cramped, wouldn't you say?'

'In a boat this size,' Rayburn said, 'it's what you have to accept. It suits us well enough. We've no complaints.'

'Well, sooner you than me. I like room to spread myself. You ready to go?'

'We are.'

'Where's the gold?'

'In the bag,' Jo said. It was lying on the settee beside her. She looped the strap over her shoulder and stood up. 'Now let's go see the Dutchman.'

She rode in the front with Carlson, the other three in the back. She kept the shoulder-bag on her lap, as if she felt the need to guard it all the way. There was not a lot of talk in the Buick. Nobody seemed to have the urge to indulge in conversation.

From Longville Carlson took the car on to the highway and headed north. There was a lot of traffic belting along in both directions, but soon he turned off to the left on to a minor road that appeared to be little used.

It was another mile or two to Blok's place. The house stood well back from the road and was approached by a winding driveway which widened on to a paved forecourt with a fountain in the middle. The house itself was built of white stone and had an imposing portico along the front. There were two storeys and in the middle of the roof was a square clock-tower.

A garage on the left looked big enough to accommodate half a dozen cars, and inside a black mechanic could be seen doing some work on a Rolls-Royce. To the right was a swimming-pool and at the rear a belt of tall Cypress trees formed a dark background and gave an indication that the surrounding ground might be swampy.

'So this is where our Mr Blok hangs out,' Jo said, as Carlson brought the Buick to a stop on the forecourt. 'Looks like he's got plenty of what it takes.'

'You can rely on that,' Carlson said. 'We'd be wasting our time coming here if he hadn't.'

'They all got out and walked towards the house, but even before they reached the portico there was a man waiting to let them in. He was a hunchback, scarcely five feet tall, black-haired, hollow-cheeked, with a thin-lipped gash of a mouth and beady eyes which peered at the visitors with more than a hint of hostility. In spite of the heat he was dressed in a black suit, as if ready to attend a funeral. Yet he did not even look warm.

He was obviously well known to Carlson, who addressed him as Jake. 'You seem to have been waiting for us.'

'Why wouldn't I be, Mr Carlson? I was warned you'd be

coming. I been on the lookout for you. Mr Blok is in the library, if you'll just come this way.'

He led them into a spacious entrance hall with a double staircase leading up to a gallery from which doors opened off. Jake avoided the stairs and conducted them to a door on the left. He rapped on the door, opened it slightly and announced with very little attempt at ceremony:

'They're here, Mr Blok. There's four of 'em.'

A throaty voice answered with a touch of irascibility: 'Well, show them in, Jake. Show them in.'

The hunchback pushed the door more widely open and indicated with a jerk of the head that they were to go inside. When they had done so he closed it on them and went away.

Blok had risen from the armchair in which he had been sitting, and he waited for Carlson to introduce the other visitors, acknowledging each introduction with a cursory nod of the head but making no move to offer a shake of the hand.

Rayburn had had a picture of the man in his mind, as one is inclined to have before meeting someone whom one knows only by name. This picture had been hazy, but in fact it had not been very far off the mark. The name had somehow made him think of a large fat man, and this was just what Blok was. He was also as bald as a coot and had a straggly ginger moustache, bad teeth and pale blue piggy eyes. He had a big cigar stuck in his mouth, and when he rolled it to one side in order to speak he sounded like someone who was permanently short of breath.

There was an Alsatian dog which had been lying on a rug close by his chair but had got up when the visitors entered, and had bared its teeth and uttered a menacing growl, as if warning them to keep their distance. Blok spoke one word to it, and it subsided on to the rug but still kept a watchful eye on the intruders. Carlson told them later that he had never seen Blok without the dog nearby, or without a cigar in his mouth except when he was eating.

'And he sure does love to eat. Else I believe he never would be without the weed. Maybe he's mastered the knack of smoking in his sleep, but I wouldn't know about that.

The library was a large room, pleasantly cool from the air conditioning. There were yards and yards of shelving stacked with books of every description. Rayburn would not have classified Blok as a literary man, so perhaps having decided that his house needed a library he had concluded that the appropriate wall-covering had to be bookshelves. The books might have been bought as a job lot just to fill the shelves. Some of them were leather-bound and appeared to be in sets. Several might have been quite valuable.

He doubted whether Blok ever read any of them, but he could have been wrong. Perhaps the man really was an avid reader. It was not a question it would have been polite, or even wise, to ask one's host.

The host himself invited the visitors to sit down. There were plenty of chairs to choose from, and he sank back into his own, which he filled to capacity.

'Nice place you have here, Mr Blok,' Laurie remarked.

'Sure, sure,' Blok said. But it was evident that he was not interested in small talk, and he got down to business straightaway. 'Roy tells me you got something to sell.'

'That's so.'

'You got it with you?'

'Miss Van Fleet has.'

Blok looked at Jo, who was sitting with the shoulder-bag on her lap. 'So I get to see it?'

'I guess so,' Jo said.

She took the gold bar from the bag, stood up and carried it across to Blok. He took it from her and held it in his pudgy hands, chewing on the cigar.

'How much you askin'?'

Rayburn said: 'We thought ten thousand dollars.'

Blok gave a derisive snort. 'Ten grand! You're crazy.'

'Well, what sort of value would you put on it?'

'A thousand would be generous.'

Rayburn had a sense of deflation and he could see that the other three were looking disappointed. Only Carlson seemed unaffected. He was lighting a cigarette and seemed relaxed, content to let the others do the talking now that he had made the introduction.

'Look, son,' Blok said, 'I ain't askin' how you came by this here gold or what claim you have to it and all that crap, though others might. And the fact is, just between ourselves I'll tell you this one bar is small beer to me. It wouldn't be worth my time bothering with if I didn't believe there's more where this came from. There is, ain't there?'

'Yes.'

'How much?'

'Quite a lot.'

Unlike Carlson, Blok was not satisfied with anything as vague as this. 'Don't muck about with me. If we're to do a deal I gotta know just how much we're talking about. Get me?'

Rayburn got him. He glanced again at his partners, seeking their opinion with a lift of the eyebrows.

'Oh, what's it matter?' Laurie said. 'Tell him.'

Neither of the girls raised any objection.

Jo shrugged. 'He's gotta know sometime.'

'That's true,' Pippa said.

Rayburn turned again to Blok. 'Ninety-seven bars.'

This revelation appeared to startle Carlson. He had obviously not expected so much. But the fat man took it with no apparent emotion.

'You goin' to tell me where the stuff is?'

'No,' Rayburn said.

Blok seemed faintly amused. 'Didn't think you would. Well, ninety-seven bars is quite some, I must admit.'

'Worth your time?'

'I'd say so.'

'So how about upping the price?'

Before Blok could answer, Carlson stood up and said: 'Can I have a word with you, Will? In private.'

Blok looked rather surprised, but he made no bones about agreeing to the request. 'Okay. I can see you got something on your mind, so I better hear what it is.'

With a certain amount of effort and some puffing and blowing, he lifted his bulk from the armchair and said; 'If you'll excuse us, ladies and gents.'

'It won't take long,' Carlson said.

They went out by a different door from that by which the visitors had entered the library. Carlson was carrying the gold bar which he had taken from Blok. The dog got up and went with them.

'Now what's our smart financial adviser up to?' Laurie said.

'Oh,' Jo said, 'I guess he's got some plan to squeeze more juice out of the Dutchman.'

The thought struck Rayburn that she was always ready to take Carlson's part. Maybe it was because she and Pippa had introduced him to them and wished to justify that introduction. Though it was noticeable that Pippa seemed less inclined to stick up for the man. He was more than a little pleased about this.

'Why couldn't he have done it in our presence?' he said.

'There could be reasons.'

'Such as what?'

'Oh, I don't know. What's biting you, anyway?'

'I don't much care for secret discussions which concern me. I like to have everything out in the open. And I don't see why he took the gold with him.'

'You worry too much,' Jo said. 'Maybe they're going to weigh it. No scales in here.'

After that not much else was said before Blok and Carlson returned, the Alsatian padding along behind. Rayburn noticed that they had not brought the gold back. Blok still had the cigar glued to his blubbery lips.

They sat down and Blok said: 'You know something? This guy's an out-and-out bargainer. He's really been putting the pressure on. And waddyer know? He's got me to agree to pay another two hundred bucks on top of the grand. I must be out of my mind.'

'I think it's a fair price,' Carlson said. 'For both sides. What you folks say?'

It was still much below what they had hoped for, Rayburn thought. But maybe it was the best deal they were likely to get.

It was Jo who answered. She said: 'I'd say it's still too damned low. But I guess we better take it.'

Nobody seemed inclined to argue about it, though nobody looked particularly gratified.

'So it's a deal? Carlson said.

'I suppose so,' Rayburn said.

And then Blok said: 'There is just one condition.'

Oh, oh! Rayburn thought. Here it comes. This is where we find there's a damned great bluebottle in the unguent. There always is.

'So what's the condition?'

'That you agree to let me have the rest of the gold at the same price.'

So the fly was not such a big one after all. None of them wanted to go round hunting for a different buyer who might possibly pay more. And the fewer people there were who knew about the gold the better.

So the deal was done. Blok handed over the cash and kept the gold bar.

There was nothing in writing, no signatures on documents. It was not that kind of deal.

8

Risk

BLOK provided lunch, and it was a good one. They ate it in a dining-room which was as big as the library. There was a long mahogany table and enough chairs for a banquet. The meal was served by a young black woman who could have walked away with the first prize in a beauty contest. She was apparently happy in her work and smiled a lot. Maybe she was generously paid; it was the sort of thing that gave people something to smile about.

The Alsatian was on hand, and Blok tossed chunks of meat to it now and then.

When they were on their way back to Fort Lauderdale Carlson told them that Blok threw parties for lots of his male and female acquaintances, and these could become pretty bacchanalian.

'You been to any of these parties?' Rayburn asked.

'A few.'

'So you mix business with pleasure?'

'I take advantage of what's on offer,' Carlson said, grinning. 'Why not? It's free.'

'Is there a Mrs Blok?'

'You kidding? Who would marry a guy like him? Except for the cash. And it's my guess he wouldn't ever let any woman get a finger on any of that. No, sir.'

'What's Jake's role? Butler?'

He had let them into the house and he had seen them out, but for the rest of the time they were there he had kept out of sight.

'I've never heard Blok refer to him as a butler,' Carlson said. 'Bit of a mystery man, our Jake. You may not have noticed, but he packs a gun under that black jacket of his.'

'I hadn't noticed. So are you saying he's a bodyguard?'

'Maybe. Doesn't look the part, but he could be a mean customer if you got on the wrong side of him.'

'He's creepy,' Jo said. 'Gives me the shivers just to look at him.'

'So don't look at him,' Carlson said.

He took them to his place to share out the money that Blok had handed over to him as their agent. His commission of twenty per cent came to two hundred and forty dollars, which left just nine hundred and sixty to be divided between the other four. So it worked out that each of them got exactly the same amount as Carlson.

When it came down to this it seemed pretty small beer, and a lot less than they had been hoping to get; but if you multiplied it by ninety-eight, the total number of ingots, it brought each share to twenty-three thousand five hundred and twenty dollars. And that, although some way short of the riches a fourth share of almost a million would have brought them, was not to be sniffed at.

'Now,' Carlson said, 'when do you propose to deliver the rest of the yellow stuff?'

'Can't be certain about that,' Rayburn said. 'Depends on a number of factors. We'll get in touch with you when we bring it in. Okay?'

Carlson grinned. 'You have to fetch it from wherever it is in the boat, don't you?'

'That's your guess?'

'Stands to reason, don't it? That's why you can't put an exact date on the delivery. My God! A boat like yours, a sail-boat with just a bit of an engine for emergencies, bringing all that gold from only you know where – it's crazy. I am right, aren't I? The stuff is seaborne.'

They just looked at him, saying nothing.

'Okay,' he said. 'So that's the way it is. So that's the way it has to be. But it's a risk. The things that could happen!'

'We've taken bigger risks,' Laurie said.

And perhaps only Rayburn knew what he was talking about. Because none of the others had been in a corvette on convoy work in the North Atlantic or on the Russia run to Murmansk. None of them could begin to imagine what it had been like, and how, after that, any voyage in *Wanderer* had to seem a cushy number in comparison.

'Well,' Carlson said, 'I just hope all goes well. For everybody's sake.'

Rayburn guessed he was thinking most of his commission. In effect he was now an equal partner with the four of them, money-wise. And it was understandable that he would have doubts regarding the dependability of one old sailing-boat as the means of transporting such a fortune in gold bullion. To him it must appear completely mad. Because gold could sink, couldn't it? It could sink like lead.

He took them back to Longville in the Buick and accompanied them on board, marvelling again at the cramped quarters in which they were happy to live.

'Guess I'd go crazy.'

'You mean you're not crazy already?' Pippa said.

'If so, it looks like it's a contagious disease. When do you aim to leave? Pretty soon, I guess.'

'Yes,' Rayburn said. 'Pretty soon.'

'Tomorrow, maybe?'

'No, not tomorrow. There are things to do when a ship's in port. Provisions to stock up on, fresh water, fuel for the engine, maintenance work. Need to relax for a while on dry land too. Anyway, there's no hurry. The stuff we're going to fetch won't run away.'

'I'm glad to hear it. You seem mighty cool, all things considered. Some guys would be all fired up.'

'Oh, he's fired up right enough,' Pippa said. 'It's just he doesn't show it. British, you know. Cold-blooded.'

'Is that a fact?'

'No,' Rayburn said. 'It's a fallacy.'

When Carlson left Jo accompanied him back to the car. A little later Rayburn went up on deck and saw them both sitting in the Buick, smoking cigarettes and apparently having a cosy tête-à-tête. When he returned to the saloon they were still there. He mentioned it to Pippa and Laurie.

'What's she got to talk to him about?' Laurie said.

He sounded peeved. It was obviously unwelcome news to him. And what Pippa had to say merely added to his displeasure.

'Oh,' she said, 'they're buddies from way back. Was a time when she was real sweet on him. Then it cooled. But maybe there's still some of that old black magic left.'

Laurie said nothing, but he looked sour.

'And how about you?' Rayburn said. 'Were you ever sweet on him too?'

'Hell, no,' Pippa said. 'Me, I never really liked the guy. Never.'

'You didn't?'

'No, I did not. I think he's a heel.'

She sounded quite vehement about it. Which pleased Rayburn.

He said: 'If he's a heel, why did you back Jo in proposing we should use him as our agent?'

'Oh that's business, isn't it? He knows his way around. And we need someone like him to shift the gold for us, don't we?'

'I think we're probably being ripped off anyway,' Laurie said.

Rayburn agreed. 'I wouldn't trust the Dutchman further than I could throw him. And at his weight, that wouldn't be far. But what's the alternative to dealing with him?'

'We could try to find another buyer.'

'But we've agreed to let him have the rest of the gold at the twelve hundred dollar price per bar. Are you suggesting we walk out on the deal? Hardly ethical.'

'If Blok is making suckers of us I don't think we should worry too much about ethics.'

'But we don't know he is.'

'Anyway,' Pippa said, 'didn't we talk about all this before? And didn't we come to the conclusion that our best bet was to work with Roy? He's sharp enough not to let the Dutchman get away with anything underhand. Sure, we'll not be getting the full market price, but in the circumstances maybe this is the best we can expect.'

'So you trust Carlson?' Laurie said.

'Oh, sure. He's a straight dealer.'

'Even if he is a heel?'

'Yes. Like I said, this is business. And that's something else again.'

She seemed quite certain about that, and the subject was dropped.

When Jo came back Laurie said: 'You had a long talk with Carlson. Was it an interesting subject?'

She must have noticed the sour note in his voice, and answered rather sharply: 'Why yes, I'd say it was. It was about money, and that's always interesting, don't you think? I told him we were not too darned happy about the price of gold.'

'And what did he say to that?'

'He said it was not at all a bad deal in the circumstances, like he'd said before. Because Blok had to make his profit and he was taking the bullion with no questions asked about the way we came by it. Which he remarked, as far as he knew, might be as illegal as all get out.'

'Well now,' Laurie said, 'that's pretty interesting in itself, don't you think? Because it means neither our Roy nor the Dutchman is above doing a deal that may not be entirely above board.'

'Aw hell!' she said. 'We all knew that already, didn't we? You surely aren't saying it's news to you, for Pete's sake, are you?'

Laurie just shrugged.

'Whoever we deal with, it's gotta be somebody that's a shade bent, if not a lot so. And at least we know Roy. We've known him quite a while.'

'You and Pippa have. Until yesterday Steve and I had never set eyes on him.'

'And you think he's a crook?'

'I didn't say that.'

'No, but you implied it.' She sounded angry. 'Well, what are you going to do about it?'

'They were thinking of trying to find a different buyer,' Pippa said.

'Now that sure would be the craziest thing. After we've come this far. And after I've persuaded Roy to try and get a better price from the Dutchman.'

'You've done that?' Laurie said.

'It's what I've been talking to him about. He thinks he may be able to put some pressure on Blok to up the ante.'

'Well, in that case—' Laurie was backing away. Jo had taken the wind out of his sails.

'In that case do you still figure we should look for a different buyer?'

'Maybe not if Carlson can really get us a better deal. Do you think he can?'

'I'd say there's a good chance. But nothing is certain.'

'Nothing ever is in this life,' Rayburn said. 'Except death.'

'Now you're being morbid,' Pippa said. 'And let's just hope that particular certainty is a long way off for all of us. Me, I've got a lot of living still to do, and I aim to enjoy it.'

'And I hope you do. But as to this question of the gold and who we sell it to, there's no need to make up our minds yet awhile. We still have to go and fetch it, and we're certainly not going to do that in a day. Or even a week.'

9

Temptation

THEY spent the next day preparing Wanderer for her return voyage to the island where the treasure was waiting for them. In addition to the usual stores they bought a spade, which would be a more suitable tool for digging than the oars they had used before.

The girls had some shopping of their own to do, and they decided to take the bus ride to Fort Lauderdale. By late afternoon neither of them had returned, and Laurie was reading a newspaper he had picked up ashore. Suddenly he gave a cry.

'Bloody hell!'

Rayburn glanced at him. 'What's up?'

'I've just come across a list of prices on the bullion market.'

'And?'

'And I'd say we've really been taken to the cleaners. Gimme a pencil and a bit of notepaper. I've got to do some sums.'

Rayburn found what was required and handed them to him. Laurie sat down at the table and did some calculations on the paper.

'Well now,' he said when he had finished, 'this is interesting. By my reckoning, which admittedly may be rough, it seems our gold bar, which we sold for twelve hundred dollars, has a market value of maybe forty-five thousand.'

'That can't be right.'

'Well, look at the figures.'

Rayburn looked at them and could find nothing wrong with the reckoning. Laurie had estimated the weight of the bar, but had probably erred on the low side if anything.

'Now why,' Rayburn said, 'didn't we look up the price before we went to Carlson?'

'Because we were daft enough to trust the man. Because we thought we would get a fair deal from him. We took the girls' word for that.'

'They must have believed it too. They've been had as well.'

'That's true. But one thing's pretty certain: Carlson knew the real value of the gold. He's in the business. So why didn't he get us a better price? It would have been more commission for him. Yet he said it was a fair offer.'

'The answer has to be that he's in with Blok. They've done a deal between themselves to fleece us and share the profit.'

'So what do we do now?'

'That's something we shall really have to think about.'

They were still thinking about it when Pippa came back – alone. It appeared that she had not seen Jo since mid-morning.

'She said she was going to get her hair done, because it was in a mess.'

'And you didn't arrange to meet her again?' Laurie asked.

'No. We had our own things to do, and there didn't seem much point. We agreed to make our own way back here when we were good and ready. Looks like her business took a bit longer than mine.'

'Well,' Rayburn said, 'we've got news for you. And I don't think you're going to like it.'

'In that case you'd better tell me and get it over with.'

He told her. And he had been right: she didn't like it.

'You're sure about those figures?'

'Well, some of it's guesswork, but if anything we think they could be low. Whichever way you look at it, we've been done down.'

'Oh, my God!' she said, and she sounded really sick. 'What are you going to do about it?'

'There's nothing we can do about that first bar. It's gone and we'll never get it back. The other lot's a different thing. We'll go and fetch it as planned.'

'And then what?'

'We haven't decided. We'll have to look for another buyer. In some different place maybe. What do you think?'

'I'll go along with anything you decide.' She frowned. 'That Roy Carlson! I knew he was a heel, but I never dreamed he'd have played a trick like this. I wonder what Jo will have to say about it. She'll have to admit he's a real son-of-a-bitch now.'

It was well on into the evening when she eventually turned up. She was carrying some plastic bags with the names of various stores on them: the harvest of her shopping.

'We were getting worried about you,' Laurie said. 'What kept you so long?'

'Oh,' she said, 'I bumped into Roy. He took me to a restaurant for lunch, and then for a spin in his car. Then we went back to his place and got to talking and – well you know how time flies.'

'Oh, sure,' Pippa said. 'And did this talking have anything to do with the price of gold?'

'Well yes, actually it did. He's been in contact with the Dutchman and he believes he's got the guy moving. Nothing definite yet, but it looks promising; it really does.'

Rayburn could tell from the expression on Laurie's face that he was not at all pleased to hear about this furher meeting between Jo and Carlson. He himself could not help feeling that the encounter seemed pretty fortuitous. He wondered whether it might possibly have been arranged the previous day when the two of them had had their talk in the Buick. Could it be, as Pippa had suggested, that some of that old black magic was being resurrected? He hoped not, because it had the potential to cast something of a blight on what had been a very happy relationship on board the yacht. If that broke up it would really sour things.

It would have given him no satisfaction at all if he had known that his suspicion regarding the meeting between Carlson and Jo was only too well founded. It had not been the result of pure chance, but had been arranged the previous day.

But he did not know this, and neither did Laurie or Pippa.

Jo had been telling the truth when she said she had had lunch with Carlson. There had, however, been not a little editing to the story of what had followed. The fact was that there had been no spin in the car; that was pure fantasy. After their lunch at one of the best restaurants in town Carlson had taken her to his house, which was unoccupied when they arrived.

A cleaning-woman, who came in daily to do the chores, had left as usual at about midday. She was a Puerto-Rican, a diligent person with an imperfect knowledge of the English language. She could get by with her limited vocabulary and a repertoire of expressive gestures, but she was completely illiterate, a fact which from Carlson's point of view was a distinct advantage, since she could not read any documents of a private nature that might be left lying around. He told people that she was a jewel. She was also young and physically attractive in a dark, Latinish kind of way. He

suspected she could be quite passionate if given any encourage-
ment, but he had never put this to the test, though it had crossed
his mind to do so on numerous occasions. The fact that she had a
husband who might be fairly passionate too, and more than a little
handy with a knife, tended to discourage him from making any
such experiment.

Jo had no husband lurking in the background, so there was
nothing to inhibit Carlson in his behaviour with her. Scarcely five
minutes after their entry into the house they were naked and sharing a refreshing shower bath. From there, having dried themselves,
it was but a step to the bedroom and a comfortable double bed,
where they diverted themselves for quite some time.

'Why,' Carlson said, 'did you and I ever split up? We were made
for each other.'

'As I recall,' Jo said, 'her name was Miriam.'

'Ah, yes. A redhead with a flaming temper. She threw a vase at
me and left in a huff.'

'I guess you deserved it.'

'Perhaps. Anyway, she was never in the same class as you.'

'Which I imagine is what you told her about me. Before she
started throwing things.'

Carlson laughed. 'Never. You're the tops.'

'Well,' she said, 'if it comes to that, you're not so bad yourself.'

'Better than the Scottie?'

She frowned slightly, as though he had touched a nerve. 'Now
let's not talk about him. Don't let's spoil the party when it's going
so nice.'

Later, when they were drinking gin and smoking cigarettes, Jo
said: 'I think we should talk some more about the gold.'

'In what way?'

'The price is not good enough, you know. The others have been
talking about looking for a different buyer.'

'But they agreed to let Blok have it all at the price he's offered. You think they might walk out on the deal?'

'I guess they might.'

Carlson was silent for a while, sucking at his cigarette and gazing thoughtfully at the girl. Then he said:

'I've got a different plan, which could be very much to your advantage.'

'Mine?' she said. 'Not the others?'

'No. Just you alone. And me too, of course. A way we'd take fifty per cent each, not twenty. Do you want to hear it?'

'I'm listening.'

'Well, for a start, it depends on you.'

'In what way?'

'You tell me where the gold is coming from.'

'Oh, I don't know about that.' She was frowning and spoke doubtfully. 'It would be like a betrayal, wouldn't it? I don't think I could do it. They trust me.'

Carlson noticed that she had not rejected the suggestion out of hand, and that was a good sign. It meant she was interested.

He said: 'There are ninety-seven more bars left. At twelve hundred per bar that comes to one hundred and sixteen thousand four hundred dollars. I've worked it all out, and twenty per cent of that comes to twenty-three thousand two hundred and eighty. That's what each of us is set to get. But fifty per cent would be fifty-eight thousand two hundred. Which I think you'll agree is a whole lot better.'

She said nothing. But she was certainly thinking about it.

Carlson said: 'My guess is you found the gold buried some-place. You've been cruising in that sail-boat, so it looks likely you went ashore here and there. There's a lot of islands scattered around; could've been one of them. Am I getting close?'

'You're close.'

'Well now, here's the idea I have in mind. The Dutchman owns a boat. It's a big motor-cruiser. Keeps it in a marina in Miami. He goes deep sea fishing in it; tuna, that sort of thing. I've been with him a few times; it's good sport. The boat's fast; much faster than anything with sails. You following me?'

'I'm following you,' she said. And it seemed she was breathing a little quicker.

'So here's the way I see it. If you were to tell us where the cache is, this island as it might be, then Blok and me, we could get there before the Limeys' boat, lift the gold and head for home.'

He stopped talking. He was looking at her, waiting for her reaction. She was frowning slightly.

'Look,' she said. 'I may be dumb, but I don't quite see how this would benefit me. Tell me.'

He told her.

'We'd strike a bargain with Blok. He takes the gold and pays us the money, the twenty per cent. You and I go halves.'

'And Pippa and the boys get nothing?'

'Somebody's got to be a loser.'

She seemed to accept that, but she was still worrying at it.

'Why would Blok go for this? He'll be getting the gold anyway. If he's going to pay the same price, where's the advantage to him?'

'Cashwise maybe no advantage, but he can't be certain your lot will deliver. He knows he's giving a poor price and he's afraid you'll find another buyer. I've told him you're thinking about it, so he doesn't feel sure he can rely on you to stick to the bargain, because he knows if he was in your shoes he wouldn't hesitate to break his word if it was to his advantage.'

'So you've talked to him about this plan of yours?'

'I've mentioned the idea to him and I think he'll buy it. The double-cross appeals to him; that's the sort of guy he is.'

She thought it might be the sort of guy Roy Carlson was too, but she did not say so.

And there was something that Carlson did not say either: that the double-cross was bigger than she could have imagined. For he and Blok knew just how much more the gold was worth than the figure that had been quoted to the finders. And they wanted the whole of it to share between themselves. They were greedy and unscrupulous, and Jo was to be their tool. The four young people had come to them like sheep begging to be fleeced, and they had been ready to oblige.

'Of course,' Carlson said, 'it all depends on you.'

'Yes,' she said, 'it does, doesn't it?'

'So what do you say? Do you want the money?'

'Now that,' she said, 'is a real stupid question. Who wouldn't, for Pete's sake?'

She had never had money; at least, never enough. She had never been able to buy all the things she would have liked to have. She had been always too dependent on other people's generosity; handouts from men who thought they owned her just because they were picking up the tab. And now here was this opportunity to have some real spending money at last. She would be a fool to reject it just because of a qualm of conscience. If Pippa had been offered a chance like this, would she have thrown it away? Well, maybe. But that was neither here nor there. It was a temptation. Oh, sure, it was a temptation all right.

But still she hesitated.

He was looking at her still, not saying anything but asking the question with his eyes.

'I don't think I can,' she said. 'It wouldn't be right.'

'It would be right for you; nothing could be more so. Just think it over. Think what you'd be throwing away if you refused.'

She did think about it; and it bothered her. She was being pulled two ways and could not make up her mind. Carlson replenished her glass with gin, and she drank it. And then they got on to the bed and made love again. And after that she drank more of the gin and was beginning to feel quite woozy, because she had never had much of a head for alcohol; it got to her very quickly.

He could see what was happening, and he said coaxingly: 'Now you are going to tell me, aren't you? You're going to tell me where the gold is and be rich.'

So then, in the end, she told him.

'It's an island. In the Bahamas. A small little island. No inhabitants. Except one. And he's dead.' She giggled. 'Just skin and bones, without the skin. Long time dead. Keeping guard.'

'This island. Does it have a name?'

'Oh, sure.'

'What is it?'

She furrowed her brow in an effort to remember, but without success.

'I forget.'

'God damn it!' Carlson said. 'Do you know how many islands there are in the Bahamas? Hundreds. We've gotta have the name. Think, Jo, think. Use what you call a brain.'

'Don't yell at me,' she said, suddenly resentful. 'I'm trying. Maybe it'll come to me.'

'It'd better. Without the name we're sunk.'

'I guess it's this gin. It's given me a woolly head.'

'So let's have a meal and see if that'll clear it.'

They showered again and got dressed and went to the kitchen which the Puerto Rican lady had left all bright and shining. Carlson brewed strong coffee and rustled up from the refrigerator the filling for sandwiches – cold roast chicken and boiled ham. They sat on stools at a counter and ate the sandwiches and drank the coffee. And after a time Jo said:

'Dove.'

'What are you talking about?' Carlson asked.

'The island. That's the name. Dove. It just came to me.'

'Are you sure?'

'Of course I'm sure. It's about the middle.'

'Middle of what?'

'The archipelago. What else? Middle of the outer fringe, if you see what I mean.'

'Right,' Carlson said. 'I'll tell Blok. He'll be able to find it on the chart. Then we'll be on our way.'

'Do I get to go with you?'

'No. You'd better stick with the others. If you were to pull out they'd be sure to want to know why. They've got to think you're still in the old partnership.'

She was not too happy about that. 'I don't see that it'd make much difference now. And I'd like to be there when you dig up the gold. I could show you were it is.'

But Carlson was adamant. It had to be played his way. 'Besides, I don't think the Dutchman would want a woman aboard.'

She wondered whether Blok had told him that. And suddenly the thought flashed into her mind that now that she had given the name of the island there was nothing to prevent the two men squeezing her out. If Roy wanted to cheat her out of her share there was no way she could force him to play the game, for she had no hold on him. But she thrust this idea away from her. She trusted him. She had to trust him. He would never betray her.

But the doubt persisted; this niggling little grain of doubt that was like a pebble in the shoe.

Have I done the right thing? she wondered. Would she live to regret that act of betrayal which she herself had perpetrated? Was she not in fact already feeling some regret? Now that it was too late.

*

Back on board the yacht she had a feeling that the others must have some suspicion that she was double-crossing them, as if it were something they might immediately guess from her manner. Surely the guilt must be apparent to them. She had to keep assuring herself that this was ridiculous; that it was sheer imagination on her part.

It was no imagination, however, that Laurie was none too happy to learn that she had spent half the day with Roy Carlson. He was jealous; that was the fact of the matter.

'It looks the same to me,' Pippa said. She had been taking a critical look at Jo.

'What does?' Jo asked.

'Your hair. That must have been the skimpiest hair-do ever.'

'I didn't have one. I decided to give it a miss.'

'No doubt the other business was more pressing,' Laurie said, with a touch of sarcasm.

She made no reply to that.

Rayburn said: 'Well, it'll have to wait now. We're leaving first thing tomorrow.'

'Oh, I didn't know that.'

'So now you do,' Laurie said. 'No more shore leave until we come back with the gold.'

'Are you going to tell Roy?'

'I don't see that it's necessary,' Rayburn said. 'He knows we're going as soon as we're ready. It'll be time to get in touch with him when we return. But I don't think we're likely to even then.'

She glanced at him sharply. 'What do you mean by that?' And then, with sudden intuition: 'Something's happened, hasn't it? That's why you've all been acting so odd. What is it?'

He answered bluntly: 'Your friend Carlson's been cheating us.'

'I don't believe it. How could he be?'

'He's in cahoots with Blok.'

She said furiously: 'It's a lie. How can you know that?'

'We've discovered the true price of gold. It's in that paper over there. And we figure that one of our bars of gold has a market value of forty or fifty grand. Even if Blok doesn't get that much, he's still taking a hefty slice of profit on what he's paying us. And Carlson's a financial wizard, isn't he? So he must know the score. He has to be doing a deal with the Dutchman.'

She wanted to deny it, but could not. She had her own doubts about him now. Maybe he was getting a lot more out of the deal than he had revealed to her; a lot more than she would be getting. But she could not alter it now; it was too late. And she could not pull out.

Nor could she warn Roy that the yacht was leaving so soon. She would just have to hope that the Dutchman would set out in his boat without too much delay. It would be the devil if *Wanderer* arrived at the island first, or even while the other lot were still loading the treasure on board. She would then be certain to be under suspicion of having given the information to Carlson regarding the location of the cache, and relations would become very strained indeed. Why could not Roy have let her go with him and Blok?

'What's up, Jo?' Rayburn asked. 'You don't look happy. Don't you want to get to sea again and lay your hands on all that lovely yellow metal?'

'Why, sure I do,' she said; and she managed to summon up a smile, thought it seemed rather forced. 'But I just can't help thinking that something might go wrong.'

'Nothing's going to go wrong. Nothing at all.'

Yet everything from his point of view was going to do just that with a vengeance.

She could have told him so, but she said nothing. From here on in she just had to let things take their course.

10

Müller

IT was some years earlier than this when a man named Heinz Müller jumped down from the back of a British army lorry and walked off to start his day's work on a small Norfolk farm.

Müller was a German and he was wearing the battledress of a prisoner of war. It was the summer of 1945, and the war in Europe was over, but it would be some time yet before Müller would be repatriated to a country that was now in ruins. Meanwhile, as a prisoner who had never been a member of the Nazi party and could be trusted not to cause trouble or try to escape, he was allowed to leave the confines of the prisoner of war camp each day to work for a farmer named Hector Wilson.

This arrangement suited Müller very well, since it was the next best thing to complete freedom, and he got on quite amicably with Mr Wilson and his wife, a middle-aged couple with no family. On the fifty-acre farm, which was of the mixed variety, partly arable and partly livestock, there was only a youth of sixteen besides the prisoner of war to assist the farmer in his daily round. There was a certain problem of communication, since the Wilsons spoke no German; but Müller had a smattering of English and quickly picked up more.

He was a small man, but stocky and quite strong, well able to handle any job on the farm, for which indeed he proved to have a natural aptitude, although he had had no previous experience of such work. Back home in a small town a few miles north of Bremen he had worked as a clerk in a lawyer's office before being conscripted. He was not sure that he would ever go back to the town, which had been practically destroyed by bombs and shells, and where, so he had learned, his parents had been killed as well as the girl he had been expecting to marry. He had been an only child and he had no relations whom he felt any desire ever to see again. He was a loner now.

He was twenty-eight years old and neither ugly nor handsome; nondescript might have been the word to describe his features. He would never have stood out in a crowd. As had been said of him, rather spitefully: once seen, never remembered. He had spiky hair, so fair one might have imagined it had been bleached, pale blue eyes which gave an impression of supreme innocence, not entirely justified, a rather snub nose and thickish lips.

Mrs Wilson, a motherly soul, thought he was such a nice boy. 'If all them Germans had been like him there wouldn't have been all the trouble there has been.'

The farmer himself, while not going quite as far as this, admitted that Müller wasn't a bad young chap. 'He's a good worker, I'll say that for him. Set him to do a job and he does it. No fuss, no hanging around.'

Müller discovered that on a small farm like this you needed to be a jack-of-all-trades. But he was a quick learner, and very soon he was feeding pigs, using a scythe, driving a tractor and even milking cows. In addition he did repair work on the somewhat dilapidated sheds that served various purposes around the place and got used to the smell of the steaming dungheap.

Very soon he was accepted as one of the family and ate his

midday meal with the Wilsons in the farmhouse kitchen, where an iron range served for all the cooking that was done and heated the water in a big copper kettle. Here he felt far more at ease than in the army hut in the prison camp, even though there he was in the company of his fellow countrymen.

He was a patient man and did not fret because of the delay in regaining his freedom. He could wait. He knew that when he returned to Germany it would be to a country ravaged and impoverished by war; a country that would have to be resurrected from the rubble. He knew that he might have difficulty in finding employment and that he might have to live from hand to mouth for quite some time. But he was prepared to face all this with resignation, because he knew that in the end he would be rich. It might take a considerable length of time to achieve this object, but the eventual outcome was not in doubt: he would most certainly be rich.

He dreamed about it. He dreamed of the day when he would lay his hands on that which he now regarded as his own. And surely he had earned the right to it. The very fact that he was still alive could only be taken as a sign that he was meant to have it; that fate had picked him out from the rest as the one most worthy to possess that wealth. There was no one else to claim it now.

In the hut where he lived with nineteen other men behind the barbed-wire fence and the locked gate he was regarded as something of an oddball who kept himself pretty much to himself. It was not that he was naturally unsociable, but he felt it advisable not to let anyone become too friendly with him. For if he did he might start exchanging reminiscences with this person who had become a friend; and then in an unguarded moment the big secret might be let out. He must not risk that; he had to keep it to himself at all costs.

There were in that hut no troublemakers; they were all men who could be trusted to work outside the camp. The army lorry picked them up in the morning and took them to their various places of employment. Then in the late afternoon it picked them up and returned them to the camp.

The dyed-in-the-wool Nazis were in a different part of the camp. They were inclined to be a sullen lot. They gathered in little groups and talked of a third world war when Germany would have regained its strength and the Nazi party would have been revived under a new Führer. They despised the moderates like Müller and had been known to make physical assaults on a few of them. Müller regarded them with distaste and just hoped the people of Germany would never again be gripped by such a madness as had possessed them during the years when Hitler was in power.

Heinz Müller had been a submariner, one of the crew of a U-boat; not by choice but simply because, having been drafted into the naval service he happened to be available when heavy losses of submarines, and more especially of their crews, had made it necessary to press more men into that most dangerous branch of the German Navy.

He hated it. He hated the cramped quarters, the claustrophobic nature of the interior of the U-boat, the sickening lack of freshness in the atmosphere when the craft was submerged, the mingled odour of engine oil, of paint and tar and a score of other ingredients, not least of which was the emanation from too many human bodies confined in too limited a space without the means of regular bathing. He hated the utter lack of privacy and the hard bunk on which he found it so difficult to sleep because of the abiding fear that never left him even in his dreams. In his imagination the U-boat was forever being depth-charged or rammed, the hull being crushed and the sea bursting in. He wondered whether his shipmates felt the same terrors. How could they not? And yet they did not show it. So perhaps to them his fears were also hidden. He tried his best to hide them, and perhaps he was successful.

Now in the safety of the prisoner of war camp or on Hector Wilson's farm he no longer had that constant nagging fear of death which had plagued his life as a submariner. But he would still awake sweating from nightmares in which he was trapped in one of those terrible steel prisons with the water gushing in.

In his waking hours, however, the chief memory was of his last trip in U.1953. He remembered the great U-boat pens at Brest, where under concrete roofs five metres thick you felt safe from the heaviest of bombs. The fifteen pens, of which five were open to the sea by way of massive steel doors, constituted a veritable underground township, with workshops, storerooms, a hospital and a powerhouse. There the U-boat was serviced and loaded with that strangest of cargoes for such a vessel: gold.

None of the crew had been told that this was what the U-boat was to carry, but it was not in the nature of things that any of them should long remain ignorant of the fact. They saw the fifty boxes marked with the swastika as they arrived, and they helped to carry them on board and stow them away. It was all very mysterious and gave rise to much guarded discussion among the crew.

This was not the only odd occurrence within twenty-four hours; nor was it the more disturbing of the two. On the previous day, without warning, a new officer arrived to take over command of the U-boat. Captain Manfred Kruger, a veteran of submarine warfare who was well regarded both by officers and ratings, was replaced by a younger man, Captain Klaus Hartmann, a complete stranger to all of them. Kruger, thus relieved of his command at a moment's notice, could do no more than introduce Hartmann to the other officers, gather his kit together and depart.

After his departure Hartmann made a little speech to the officers assembled in the wardroom. He was a man of less than thirty and must have had a swift rise to his present rank. He had fair, closely cropped hair and was handsome enough to be attractive to women, if not to this particular audience, who listened in silence to what amounted to little less than a harangue. He spoke of their duty to the Führer and the Fatherland and the need for strict discipline at all times. He concluded by clicking his heels, giving the Nazi salute and uttering the words: 'Heil Hitler!'

None had ever heard Captain Kruger address them in this way, and they were slow to respond. Hartmann was obviously expecting them to do so in the appproved style, and after some hesitation each of them gave the salute and spoke the words, perfunctorily and with some reluctance.

Hartman frowned but made no remark. It was not difficult to read in his expression, however, that he was not satisfied with this response.

It was very soon realized by officers and crew alike that with the assumption of command by Klaus Hartmann a new régime had been established on board; stricter, less relaxed, more National Socialist in character. For Hartmann was without doubt a fanatical Nazi, which was possibly the reason why he had been appointed to take command of the U-boat at this time. Kruger, who had never been a party member, might have been regarded as a man not entirely to be trusted to carry out this particular mission, which the arrival of the cargo so soon after that of the new captain seemed to indicate would be somewhat different from the usual kind.

Only Hartmann knew from the outset what the nature of that mission was. He had been briefed at a somewhat unusual conference in Berlin before being flown to Brest. It had been impressed upon him that the utmost secrecy was essential and that not before the U-boat was at sea was he to reveal the substance of his orders to the other officers. He carried out these instructions to the letter; he would never have thought of doing otherwise; and he descended upon the unsuspecting ship's company like a blight.

That he was a singularly unlikeable man, who in a very few days had succeeded in antagonizing everyone else on board, was neither here nor there. Though he could not have been unaware of the fact, it did not appear to trouble him. Possibly he revelled in the knowledge, regarding it as a tribute to his character and taking a delight in imposing his will on that little company of men confined within the curved steel walls of the U-boat.

Müller was one of these men, and he felt that the substitution of this bloody-minded Nazi for the decent easygoing Captain Kruger made life on board harder to bear even than it had been before. When the great steel doors opened to let the vessel slip out from the safety of the pen he wondered just what lay ahead, and whether this would prove to be that fatal voyage from which he would never return.

So far he had been lucky. You had to be to stay alive in the U-boat service. There had been two happy times, so-called: one had been when the enemy had not had bombers with a long enough range to cover the gap in the middle of the Atlantic, that black hole. There the wolf-packs had lain in wait for the convoys and had made a killing. But later the gap had been closed with long-range aircraft and it had not been so good. Then, however, there had been the second happy time when the Americans entered the war, and ships, tankers especially, coming north unescorted from the Gulf of Mexico, were silhouetted at night against the lights of the towns along the eastern seaboard. They were picked off like flies.

But it did not last long. The Americans learned to use the convoy system and the towns were blacked out. Now there was no happy time anywhere, and U-boats were being sunk at such a rate that it was said a soldier on the Russian front had more chance of survival than a crew member in one of those death-traps.

Müller hoped the war would soon be over, but he feared it would last for some time yet. He had no doubt about the eventual outcome. Germany would lose. Things were going badly in the east, and it was common knowledge that the Allies were preparing for an invasion of France. The only question to be answered was: where would they strike? Bombers had been pounding the Pas de Calais for months but this might be bluff, simply a diversion to mask their true intentions. There was much activity along the English south coast, and there had been a story going round that E-boats had made a night-time interception of unescorted ships and landing craft packed with troops, apparently on a beach storming exercise. The E-boats had attacked and caused considerable destruction and loss of life.

Müller was not sure how much truth there was in this story, but things were certainly happening and the invasion could not be far away. And then maybe the end of this wretched war might just be in sight.

The question that most concerned him was: would he live to see it?

11

Milch Cow

IT was growing dark when U-1953 slipped down Le Goulet Channel and into the Atlantic Ocean. She ran westward submerged until well clear of land, then surfaced in the darkness and continued on the same course for some two hundred miles before turning to port and heading south. No navigation lights were showing, and at all times a sharp lookout was kept for any shipping.

It was not, however, intended that the U-boat should attack any vessel that might be sighted. Hartmann had by this time acquainted his officers with the real purpose of the voyage.

'We are to travel south to a rendezvous off the coast of Argentina. There a motor-launch will take on board our cargo and transport it to land.'

'And what happens to it after that?' Lieutenant Spranger inquired.

'That is not our concern. We have no further interest in it. And I may say it is none of your business.'

Hartmann spoke sharply, but Spranger was not easily put off. He was older than his present captain and more experienced; a blunt, outspoken man who might have attained a higher rank if he had been less independent and more tactful with superiors; or even if he had known the right sort of people – those with influence.

'But I think it is my business,' he said. 'I think it's the business of everyone taking part in the exercise. Why would a load of gold bullion be sent to a country at the other end of the earth? For what purpose?'

One of the engineer officers, a man named Gerhardt Merkel, a slouching, unkempt character, always smelling of oil and strong pipe tobacco, suggested that it was perhaps going to pay for munitions.

Spranger dismissed this idea. 'Munitions from Argentina! Hardly likely. They're buyers, not sellers in that line.'

'Beef, then.'

'Beef? And how would it be shipped to Germany?'

Merkel shrugged, having apparently exhausted his list of suggestions.

Spranger said: 'My guess is that somebody high up, maybe a group of them, is putting something away for the future. Maybe there's an escape route to South America all mapped out. It could be insurance, so that if things go really wrong there'll be this nest egg waiting.'

'What do you mean, if things go really wrong?' Hartmann spoke icily. 'You are surely not suggesting that Germany may lose the war?'

'It is a possibility, to put it no higher, don't you think?'

Hartmann reddened. 'I will not have such defeatist talk in this wardroom. I will not permit anyone on board to say such things. And there is to be no further discussion regarding the purpose of this mission. Is that understood?'

'If you wish, Captain.'

'I do wish. It is an order. Acquaint the crew.'

It was an order that even Hartmann could not enforce. The matter was discussed endlessly, both by officers and ratings, but never within the hearing of the captain. He might have suspicions that his order was not being obeyed, but he had no proof. Of one thing he could not be unaware, and this was the dislike, even hostility, which he aroused in everyone on board. Yet it did not seem to affect him. The fact was that he felt himself so superior to everyone else that he regarded his virtual isolation, mental if not physical, with a certain satisfaction. He knew what his orders were and why he had been the one chosen to carry them out; it was because it was he alone who could be trusted to do so to the letter. That was a responsibility he felt proud to bear.

The basic fact was that he knew what his duty was as a patriotic German. It was to serve the Führer, to serve the Party and to serve his country. When he thought of this he mentally clicked his heels, gave the Nazi salute and uttered those talismanic words: 'Heil Hitler!'

As Spranger remarked to Gerhardt Merkel. 'The man's not right in the head.'

Merkel agreed. 'And we're stuck with him.'

They were three days out when another subject drove all discussion of the gold and its ultimate purpose into temporary retirement. Signals were being picked up that American, British and Canadian troops had stormed ashore on the beaches of Normandy. The invasion of Europe had begun.

Müller's heart leaped. So it had come at last; it had really come at last. And perhaps it would not take so very long to finish the job so that they could all go home. But meanwhile of course he was still confined in this damned steel prison, which might yet be sent to the bottom of the sea.

So his initial feeling of delight was soon quenched and he was saddened by the thought of how many of his countrymen would have to die before the end arrived. Would not the sensible course be to surrender at once and save further bloodshed on both sides? But of course Hitler would never sanction that; the madman would fight on until everything had been destroyed.

Hartmann was contemptuous. 'They will be slaughtered like cattle. It will be another Dieppe. The beaches will be running with blood, but it will not be German blood. Our guns will tear them to pieces.'

Spranger was of a different opinion. 'Dieppe was a long time ago. They'll have learnt their lesson. This time they'll have built up an overwhelming force, and they'll have superiority in the air. It won't be easy to dislodge them once they've got a foothold.'

'Even if they get past the beaches our panzers will take care of them.'

'They've got tanks too. They know what they're doing.'

'So you think all is lost just because the enemy has landed some men on a Normandy beach?' Hartmann spoke sneeringly. 'That is a very feeble way of looking at it. I hope our troops manning the coastal defences have more spirit than that.'

'It may take more than spirit,' Spranger said.

They were standing in the conning-tower and the U-boat was forging ahead on the surface at a steady fifteen knots. It was warm; the sun was shining from an almost cloudless sky and the sea was calm. Conditions could hardly have been better, and it was all so peaceful that it was difficult to imagine the scene of carnage on those beaches far away to the north. Spranger, scanning with his binoculars that wide circle of water enclosed by the faintly etched merging of sea and sky which formed the horizon, could discern no other craft of any description. Which was just the way they wished it to be.

'I suppose,' he said, 'this will make no difference to us? We will still proceed on our mission?'

'In the absence of new orders, yes. I don't see why there should be any alteration.'

'I suppose not,' Spranger said. And indeed he could see that if he was correct in his belief that the gold was being shipped to Argentina as a form of insurance against a German defeat, whoever it was who had arranged the operation would have all the more reason to see it go ahead now that the Allied invasion of France had brought the possibility of the defeat so much closer. 'Let us hope there is no unfortunate incident to interrupt our progress.'

Hartmann said tartly: 'I see no reason why there should be. Do you?'

Spranger shrugged. 'Do such incidents need a reason?'

Neither of them mentioned what kind of incident they were referring to. It was not necessary. They both knew.

It soon became apparent from further signals which were being picked up that Hartmann's confidence that the invasion of Normandy would quickly be repulsed by the German defenders was misplaced. Slaughter there had been, but beachheads had been established and the invaders were pressing on inland. Hartmann stubbornly refused to believe in the possibility of defeat, but he spoke very little about the situation in Europe. He had become taciturn, tight-lipped, frowning a great deal. If any of the officers broached the subject in his presence he would tell them brusquely that he did not wish to discuss the matter and any speculation regarding the ultimate outcome of the conflict was pointless, since Germany was bound to be victorious in the end.

Naturally, this failed to discourage others from discussing the subject when he was not close enough to overhear them, and speculation was rife in the seamen's quarters. There the general opinion was that now that the invaders had got a foothold on the mainland, the game was up and that the terrible destruction of U-boats and the crews who manned them was now in sight. Petty Officer Georg Borchert, a crusted individual getting on for forty and as tough as they came, voiced the general opinion when he said that enough was enough.

'It's been going on too long. And the longer it gets, the worse it gets. And where's the sense in it? That's what I'd like to know. Who's going to gain by it when all's said and done? Not us, that's for certain.'

Müller had never expected to hear Borchert express such an opinion as this. It would not have pleased Captain Hartmann if he had heard it. But the petty officer was sensible enough to make sure that Hartmann was not within earshot; and he must have felt quite sure none of those who heard him would carry tales to the captain. They all preferred to have as little to do with him as possible.

There was an earlier rendezvous to keep before that with the Argentine boat. This was at a point in the ocean some two hundred miles east of the Leeward Islands in the West Indies, and the meeting was with a tanker U-boat, one of the so-called milch cows which were used to refuel ordinary U-boats and increase their endurance. There were few of them left now, but this one was still around. The sea was dead calm, and everything seemed to be going smoothly for the enterprise so far, the outward voyage up to this point having been without incident.

Seeing the milch cow, Spranger could not help reflecting on the amount of organizing that must have gone into this business of shifting a load of gold from Europe to Argentina. He still clung to his belief that it was being shipped out for someone who had made arrangements for an escape route if matters came to the worst. But it had to be someone really high up; someone with great influence, whose orders would be obeyed without question. He could think of only one man as powerful as that, apart of course from the Fuhrer himself, who could be ruled out. This man was Admiral Karl Doenitz, Commander-in-Chief of the German Navy.

As soon as the thought came into his mind he dismissed it. He could not believe it. It shocked him even to think about it. It had to be somebody else. A syndicate perhaps. A group of party big-wigs. The choice was wide. Nevertheless, it was certain that Doenitz had the authority – and he was a U-boat man. Though of course that meant nothing. But Doenitz was an honourable man; he surely would not stoop to anything like this; it was unthinkable.

And where did the gold come from? How had it been obtained? From the Jews? Perhaps. But all this was pure speculation. And might not Hartmann have been right after all? Might it not be a Government operation, fully approved and completely above board? Possibly. But he still did not believe it. He preferred to believe the other idea.

The captain of the milch cow was a man named Gans. He was a big fat man with a paunch, who looked as though he might have put away many a mug of beer in his time. He was wearing dirty white shorts and a short-sleeved shirt, with nothing on his feet, which were dirty too. His hair was blond and he spoke with a coarse Bavarian accent.

When the flexible pipe had been connected up and oil was being pumped from milch cow to U-boat, he invited Hartmann to step aboard the tanker and have a drink with him.

'A glass of schnapps will be good for the throat, eh?'

The prospect of drinking with this slovenly individual held no great appeal for Hartmann, but he hesitated to offend Gans by rejecting the invitation. So he crossed over to the deck of the other boat and followed Gans down to the quarters.

There was no U-boat in service that had accommodation to rival even a third-rate hotel. There were too many men confined in too limited a space. But this one beat all that Hartmann had come across for slumminess. In the officers' messroom Gans produced a half-full bottle of schnapps and a pair of glasses which he polished with a grimy rag that did service as a teacloth.

'So,' he said, 'we've got a second front on our hands. As if we didn't have enough trouble with the gottam Russkis.'

'We can handle both,' Hartmann said.

'You think so?'

'Of course.'

'You're one big optimist, I think. Me, I'd say it's all over now. Sure, we'll go on fighting, but it'll be a losing battle. There's too much stacked against us.'

'That is defeatist talk. You should not say such things.'

'I speak the truth. So maybe I am a defeatist, but I am also a realist. When the writing is on the wall I don't just close my eyes; I read it and take notice. And here it is all very plain to see if you are not a blind man.'

Gans lifted his glass of schnapps, took a swig and smacked his lips. Hartmann regarded him with distaste. Everything about the man offended him: the gross sweating body, the slovenly shorts and shirt, the dirty bare feet, the hairy chest, the facial stubble. And now, most of all, this talk of a German defeat. A man could be shot for that; it was treason.

He told Gans so, and the remark was greeted with mocking laughter. 'So who will shoot me? You? Do not be so starchy, Captain. Look at things as they are. Three, four years ago all is fine. We take Poland, France, Belgium, Holland, Denmark, Norway; it is easy. Only that damned island scross the water is not so easy. Then we attack Russia, and that is one big mistake. Oh yes, that is just too big a mouthful to swallow. It is a damn fool thing to do.'

Hartmann could hardly contain his anger. 'You dare to challenge the Führer's judgement?'

'Don't you?'

'No,' Hartmann almost shouted the word. 'Never.'

'Then, Captain,' Gans said, 'I am sorry to say it, but you are a fool.'

Hartmann stood up, pale with fury, controlling himself only by a supreme effort. 'I must go. There are matters to attend to.'

'But you have not touched your schnapps.'

Hartmann felt an urge to throw the liquor into Gans's face, but he did not. He saw now that it had been a mistake to accept the man's invitation in the first place. The sooner the refuelling operation was completed, the better.

12

The Plan

DESPITE the somewhat acrimonious termination of the tête-à-tête between the two captains, the refuelling of the U-boat proceeded without a hitch. As soon as it was completed the flexible pipe was unlinked and the hawsers holding the two craft together were cast off. The U-boat's engines came to life and she moved away from the milch cow.

Captain Gans, standing barefooted in his grubby deshabille and with a sardonic grin on his unshaven face, gave a perfunctory and half-mocking Nazi salute. Hartmann, rigidly at attention in the conning-tower, returned this farewell gesture with one that might have been a rebuke to the other man in its perfect execution: right arm thrust stiffly out from the shoulder at exactly the correct angle, hand palm down, fingers outstretched, left hand flat upon his waist where the buckle of the Sam Browne belt would have been if he had been wearing one.

'Heil Hitler!'

And Gans laughed. It was the final insult. Hartmann, with rage in his heart, just hoped that some avenging angel in the shape of a British or American destroyer would sink the milch cow, taking with it to the bottom of the sea this perfidious swine of a sea captain. That such a wish might in itself be a kind of treason did not occur to him.

Soon the U-boat, once again on course for Argentina, had left the tanker out of sight and was alone on a shimmering sea. Captain Hartmann, his anger having cooled, felt satisfied that all was going according to plan. Gans had called him a fool, but even he could never have suspected that his guest was living in a fool's paradise and that very soon he would discover that matters were most certainly not proceeding in the way he might have expected.

For the fact was that in secret, under his very nose as it were, a plot had been hatched; a plot which promised to alter the entire character of the operation.

It had its origin in the mind of one, Julius Spranger, that most senior of the officers under his command. From Spranger it had passed to Jacob Fischer, the senior engineer officer, and thence to Gerhardt Merkel. Very soon all the officers except the captain himself were involved. Then it spread by way of Petty Officer Georg Borchert to the ratings, until no one other than Hartmann was unacquainted with it. And even if not every man was whole-heartedly in favour of the proposed course of action, no one was hardy enough to stand out against it or to tell Captain Hartmann what was afoot. The fact that everyone detested the man had much to do with this reticence; while there was also the attraction of the plan itself and the lure of something that no one could honestly say he did not desire.

In essence the plot was simple. It could be outlined in very few words, thus: Take the gold and share it out between them.

Spranger, the original begetter of the scheme, put the argument in favour of it in rather more words.

'It's a thousand to one that the gold is going to feather the nest of some rat that's preparing to leave the sinking ship. Because there's nothing Argentina can sell to Germany that would make the least bit of difference to the course of the war. So why should we all put our lives on the line to furnish a safe haven for some bastard or bastards like that? Why not take the loot for ourselves?'

Fischer was in entire agreement with this when it was put to him. 'But how can we do it? We can't just take the gold and make a run for it. We're at sea, aren't we?'

Patiently Spranger outlined his plan, and Fischer began to see how it could be done; how they could take the gold and at the same time ensure that they did not lose their lives while the war dragged on to its inevitable conclusion.

Fischer thought it a good plan, and could see no reason why it should not be successful. Like Spranger said, the plot was simple, as all the best plots were; the fewer complications there were, the less chance there was of anything going wrong.

'First we take over the boat. Hartmann can't stop us if we have everyone else with us.'

'You're talking of mutiny,' Fischer said. 'Can we carry them all with us?'

He did not say that he himself was against the idea. 'Suppose some of them side with the captain?'

'Is it likely? Do they love him that much?'

'But mutiny. And in wartime. You know what the punishment for that is.' Fischer drew the edge of his hand along his throat in a graphic gesture. 'Might scare them off, that sort of prospect.'

'But it'll never come to that. When this war ends there'll be chaos in Germany. There'd be nobody to put us on trial even if we were there; which we won't be. And besides, it's not only the gold that'll be an attraction. Think of the joy of escaping from this hellish U-boat service where the odds against your living to tell the tale are so damned long it doesn't bear thinking about. So who's going to turn down the chance of getting out of it with a whole skin and just sitting out the rest of the war in safety and comfort?'

'Now tell me how we're going to manage that,' Fischer said.

Spranger told him.

'After we've seized the boat we turn around and head for the Bahamas. There are hundreds of islands in the group and most of them are uninhabited. We pick one of these, take the gold ashore and bury it. Then we take the boat to Brazil and ask for asylum.'

'We'll be interned.'

'Maybe we will and maybe we won't. They're pretty easygoing in that country, so I've heard.'

'Well, if we're not interned and they let us stay, what do we live on?'

'We can take a little of the gold with us. Enough to see us through. After the war is over we get a boat, pick up the rest and share it out.'

'Why not take the lot to Brazil in the first place?'

'Might lead to complications. Safer this way.'

Fischer thought about it for a while. Then he said: 'You've left out one thing.'

'What's that?'

'Hartmann. What do we do about him?'

'We could invite him to join us.'

'You must be joking.'

'No. We have to give him the chance.'

'He'll never take it.'

'Well, that's up to him. It's his choice.'

'And if he refuses?'

'We'll have to think about that.'

Müller was completely in favour of the plan. It not only held the promise of a share in the gold but, which was perhaps even more attractive, it promised an escape from the U-boat; from the squalor of life on board and the constant fear of death. This way he would be assured, not only of surviving the war, but of coming out of it with a considerable sum of money with which to make a fresh start in life.

To him it seemed that the proposed course of action was just perfect in every way, and he could not understand why some of his shipmates should have hesitated to back it; for most of them were conscripts like himself and hated the service as much as he did. However, after much whispered discussion and seeing that the majority were strongly in favour of the idea, they all cast their doubts aside and fell in with the rest.

The example of Petty Officer Borchert contributed much to this conversion of the waverers. He argued the case for backing the plan very stoutly indeed, and since he was an older and more experienced man, his arguments carried weight.

'But,' one of the men said, 'some of us have wives and families. What about them?'

'All the more reason,' Borchert said, 'for doing what's proposed. We'll be alive and we'll be going back with money in our pockets. Think how glad they'll be to see us.'

He did not add: 'If they themselves are alive.' But it was in his mind. He himself had a wife and kids in Dresden. But he felt sure they were safe enough. No one would bomb Dresden, would they?

They were swayed by him, and even before the rendezvous with the U-tanker the matter was settled. Only Hartmann remained ignorant of what was going on. A more sensitive man might have detected a certain tension in the boat, an air of expectation. He might have asked questions, quizzed his officers, tried to get to the bottom of it. Hartmann detected nothing and asked no questions. He fancied he had the entire complement of officers and ratings under his thumb. He flattered himself that in the brief time he had been on board he had introduced a discipline that had obviously been lacking under the former captain; and if in so doing he had made himself unpopular, so be it; this did not bother him in the least. He was not looking for popularity, especially if the only way to gain it was by relaxing his grip and allowing slackness to creep back in.

As the U-boat moved steadily southward, only that business with the gross Captain Gans niggled slightly. He wondered whether on his return to Brest he ought to report the matter. Gans ought to be reprimanded; he had been most insulting; even worse, he had had the temerity to question the Führer's judgement. But was it really worth bothering oneself about such a man? Perhaps not. Perhaps best to dismiss him from one's mind and concentrate on the job in hand.

Having come to this conclusion, Captain Hartmann felt a degree of satisfaction, as though he had, mentally at least, put Captain Gans firmly in his place and need not trouble himself any further with the man.

And as things turned out, he very soon had another matter to exercise his mind; a matter that was both unexpected and most unwelcome.

13

Man of Honour

IT started when Julius Spranger asked if he could have a word with Hartmann in private.

'There is something I have to discuss with you, Captain. It is most important.'

Hartmann looked surprised and somewhat displeased. 'I cannot think what there can be for us to discuss. Important, you say?'

'I am sure when you hear what it is you will agree that it is very much so.'

Hartmann, after a brief hesitation, apparently decided that there was no way he could reasonably refuse to agree to the request, and he said: 'Oh, very well then. We'd better go to my cabin.'

Even the captain's cabin on board the U-boat was extremely cramped; yet it accurately reflected the character of its occupant. Spranger remembered what it had been like when Captain Kruger had had it. Then there had been a general impression of untidiness about it: sea boots flung down in a corner, clothing thrown on the bunk, a reek of pipe smoke in the air . . . Hartmann did not smoke, and in the cabin now there seemed to be a place for everything and everything in its place. But it was less welcoming; as was the man whose retreat it was, and who now spoke in a snappish, impatient manner.

'Well, out with it. What is this important matter that you wish to discuss? I suppose it concerns me?'

'Oh, indeed, yes. It concerns you very closely.'

'In what way?'

'In a very fundamental way. As I think you will agree when you hear what it is.'

Hartmann made a gesture of impatience. 'So why are you not saying at once what it is? I am listening.'

'Captain Hartmann,' Spranger said, 'I have to inform you that you are no longer in command of this vessel.'

Hartmann stared at him. 'Have you taken leave of your senses?'

'Not at all.'

'Then what is the meaning of this nonsense? If there is a meaning.'

'Oh, there is, I assure you. And it is not nonsense. Do you notice something? Something a little odd.'

'What are you talking about?'

'I am talking about the motion of the boat. I would say we are changing course, wouldn't you?'

Hartmann was astounded. Now that it had been mentioned to him, he could detect that the U~boat was making quite a drastic alteration in course.

'What is happening? I have given no order.'

'Of course not,' Spranger said. 'Did I not tell you that you are no longer in command? Therefore, you are not giving the orders any more. It is a little unfortunate for you, but that is the way it is.'

'You are mad,' Hartmann said. 'I will go and see what the meaning of this is. And you, my friend, will be in deep trouble. Get out of my way.'

Spranger did not move. He said: 'No, Captain. It is you who are in trouble. You must not imagine that I am acting on my own. If you leave this cabin you will discover that everyone on board is against you. Stay here for the present. Sit down and listen to me while I tell you what the situation is.'

'I will not sit down.' Hartmann spoke angrily. 'I refuse to listen to what you have to say. Now let me pass. By what right do you tell me what to do?'

'By the right of this perhaps,' Spranger said. He took from his pocket a Walther automatic pistol. He did not point it at Hartmann; there was no need to do so. But the threat was there. 'Now will you sit down?'

Hartmann stared at the gun. He knew that it was the only firearm on board the U-boat, and he knew also that it should have been in a locker in that very cabin. A locker that was never in fact locked.

'You took my pistol. You sneaked in here behind my back and took it from the locker.'

'No,' Spranger said, 'not I. One of the seamen.'

'On your orders?'

'On the orders of the committee. It seemed to be a sensible precaution. You might have been tempted to do something rash.'

'Committee?'

'We believe in doing things in a democratic manner. We have had enough of dictators, great or small. Now will you sit down?'

Hartmann did so, looking angry and bemused.

'So this mutiny?'

'Oh, let us not use harsh words. It is the will of the majority – unanimous in this case – making itself felt.'

'Have you thought what will happen to you when you return to Germany? You will not be treated leniently; you may be sure of that.' Hartmann spoke sneeringly. 'You may not be so happy when the gun is at your head or the rope about your neck.'

Spranger gave a smile. 'But my dear Captain, we shall not be returning. At least, not until this wretched war is over. And by that time there will not be any court in Germany bothering itself with a handful of returning exiles.'

'Ah, now I see what you are relying on. You are like that fellow Gans we have just left. You think the Fatherland will be defeated.'

'Gans thinks that too, does he?'

'Yes. I told him he was a defeatist and could be shot for such talk.'

'What did he say to that?'

'He laughed. He is a pig. A brainless swine.'

'Perhaps he has more brains than you imagine.'

'Like you, eh?' Hartmann was sneering again. 'You think you are very clever now – with a gun in your hand. But you are heading for a fall. You cannot hope to get away with this.'

'Oh, but I do hope to. I am confident of it. And you will have to admit that these hopes are well founded when I tell you what we propose to do.'

'The first thing being this alteration in the boat's course.'

'Just so.'

They could tell by the motion of the boat that the manoeuvre had been completed and that they were back on an even keel.

'And where are we heading now?'

'To the Bahamas.'

Hartmann made no effort to hide his astonishment. 'The Bahamas! For what purpose?'

'We intend to bury the gold on one of the uninhabited islands in the group.'

'Bury it! Now I know you are mad. How the devil will that help you?'

'We shall know where it is when the time comes to dig it up again.'

'And when will that be?'

'When the war is over.'

'And in the meantime you sail the seas like The Flying Dutchman. Is that it?'

'No, of course that is not it. And I don't think you supposed it was. We're not really mad, you know. We have thought this out.'

'Very well. So you've buried the gold on this desert island. What next?'

'We take the boat to Brazil and give ourselves up. You see the advantage, don't you? No more discomfort of living in a damned iron tube full of machinery and truck of every kind, including a lot of stinking human bodies; no more existing in constant fear of a particularly unpleasant way of dying; no more eating this filthy U-boat food; no more seeing the same old faces day after day, listening to the same old voices saying the same old things. Goodbye to all that. Think of it, man; think of it. Doesn't it make your heart beat faster? And the women in Brazil; they're really something, so I've been told.'

Hartmann looked at him stonily. 'I am a married man. I love my wife.'

'Well, cut out the women. But the rest of it; doesn't that attract you? The money, the easy living, the knowledge that you can be sure of surviving the war.'

'Surely,' Hartmann said, and he sounded as though he could hardly believe what he had heard, 'you are not inviting me to join you.'

'And why not? It would avoid any – what should I say? – unpleasantness. Don't you see?'

'What I see,' Hartmann said, 'is a traitor inviting me to join him in his treachery. You insult me by even suggesting I would consider it for one moment.'

'And nothing will make you change your mind?'

'Nothing.'

Spranger sighed. 'I was afraid you might refuse. But you cannot say you were not given the chance. Now I must go and tell the others. I don't think it will come as any great surprise to them. You are a stubborn man, Captain.'

'I am a man of honour. It seems that you have none.'

'Well, that is a matter of opinion.'

Spranger turned and left the cabin.

When he had gone Hartmann sat for a while perfectly motionless, trying to come to terms with the situation. How, he asked himself, could he have been so blind to what was going on under his very nose? But they had been clever; not one of them had given any hint of what was afoot. And what reason had he had to suspect anything? Who could have foreseen anything so completely unimaginable as this? That all these men under his command should have conspired to betray their captain, to betray their country and above all to betray the Führer! An entire ship's company of traitors with but one exception; and that one now rendered powerless to oppose in any effective way the carrying out of this criminal plan.

He was seized with fury at the thought of it, of the way he had been rendered so impotent. How they must all be laughing at him! But it was no laughing matter. At least, not for him.

And then he remembered that word Spranger had used: unpleasantness. At the time he had given it little thought, had let it pass without comment. But now it came back into his mind with an almost physical jolt. For he saw that it could have a very sinister meaning; and a shiver ran down his spine. For could the plotters allow him simply to walk away from them when, as they planned, they went ashore in Brazil? Not if he were not himself implicated; since there would be nothing then to prevent him from reporting the crime to Berlin and making it impossible for these men to show their faces ever again in their native country for fear of being arrested on a most serious charge; one that included not only mutiny on the high seas but also the theft of a fortune in gold bullion belonging to the State.

Spranger, of course, professed to believe that Germany would be defeated and that in the ensuing chaos the crime they had committed would never be dealt with. But none of them could be certain of this, and they would not feel safe as long as there was a potential informer running free.

So there came again that shiver down the spine, and Captain Hartmann began to feel very much alone and very much in danger.

But what could a man of honour do? What but stick to his guns? No compromise!

14

Guardian

THEY had surveyed a number of islands with the aid of binoculars before they came to one that appeared to be eminently
suitable for their purpose.

'This is it,' Spranger said. 'This is surely it.'

No one disagreed. They felt sure it would be hard to find any
better place.

There was a small bay, a coral reef some distance away to starboard, a sandy beach, almost white under the hot sun, palm trees
beyond the beach. The entire length of this piece of land was not
more than a quarter of a mile from north to south, and probably
less from east to west. It was too small for human habitation; too
small for anything perhaps except the burial of stolen treasure.

'It'll do,' Fischer said. 'No point in any further search.'

Hartmann had come up on deck. No restraint had been put on
his movements since command of the U-boat had been taken from
him. In a way he had become a nonentity, an irrelevance, largely
ignored. With the ratings he had no contact at all, and with the officers very little. No one spoke to him regarding the operation that
was taking place, and if he broached the subject he got no response.
As far as they were concerned it seemed there was nothing to

discuss. In effect it was as if he no longer existed, and he could not help wondering gloomily how long it would be before the fantasy changed to fact.

The U-boat was steered at dead slow speed into the bay and carefully manoeuvred into a position where the bows nosed gently into the firm sand of the curving beach. The engines were stopped and the boat lay motionless with the water lapping gently at its sides.

'So far,' Spranger remarked, 'so good.'

The tide was going out, and after a time it was possible for a man to lower himself from the bows with the aid of a rope and stand in water no higher than his thighs. It was time to start unloading the cargo.

One after another the boxes containing the gold were brought up from below, carried forward and lowered to the men now standing in the water and waiting to receive them. From there they were transported up the gently sloping beach to a spot near the trees which had been chosen for their burial. One box only had been left on board.

For use as improvised spades for the digging, some boards had been ripped off crates that had originally held provisions. They were not ideal tools for the job, but the sand was not hard and it was felt that there was no need for a very deep hole. A fairly thin layer of sand covering the boxes would be enough, since it was unlikely that anyone would come to the island and start digging around in the hope of finding buried treasure. They themselves would be the next to dig there when they returned to claim their gold.

Hartmann, bareheaded and wearing a short-sleeved shirt, shorts and a pair of canvas shoes, was an interested observer of what was going on, but he took no hand in it. He did, however go ashore; not from choice but because he was ordered to do so.

'It will be good for you to stretch your legs,' Spranger told him.

'I have no wish to stretch my legs,' Hartmann said.

'It is of no consequence what you wish. This is an order.'

'And if I refuse?'

'Don't make things difficult. Do you wish us to use force? We can if necessary, but it would be undignified and the result would be the same. One way or another, you must go ashore.'

'In order to save you the bother of carrying my dead body to the grave when you've killed me. Is that it?'

Spranger affected surprise. 'Who said anything about killing you?'

'No one. But it is obviously what you intend. I am not a fool. I realize you can't permit me to stay alive, knowing what you have done. A live Klaus Hartmann would always be a threat.'

'There is something in what you say,' Spranger admitted. 'But I assure you we have no intention of killing you. It will not be necessary.'

His meaning dawned on Hartmann gradually. 'Ah! I see how it is. You intend to leave me here; to maroon me. On this barren island it will be as effective as a bullet or a knife. But it will ease your conscience. You will be able to maintain that you have not shed my blood. What a sophist you are!'

'You still have the choice. You could still throw in your lot with us.'

'And become a traitor myself? Never! Never, damn you!'

'Very well. If you are adamant there is no more to be said. You must come ashore with me.'

Hartmann made no more resistance. Accompanying Spranger, he moved to the bows and lowered himself into the water, which was now no more than knee-deep. Together the two men walked up the beach to where the digging of the cache was almost completed. Forty-nine boxes of gold had been brought ashore and were now stacked in a pile, waiting to be buried. It had been decided finally to retain just the one box for possible expenses in Brazil.

Some of the men glanced at Hartmann, and he felt he could read what was passing in their minds. To them he must already seem like a dead man, for they knew he was to be left on the island to die of thirst. Maybe they would leave him some fresh water, but if so it would only serve to prolong the agony. He could finish things by swimming out to sea until his strength failed and he could swim no longer. The possibility that some vessel might come within sight of the island in the next few days and that his signals would be noticed was too remote to give any hope. No, there was nothing that would save him. He was a dead man, sure enough.

He walked away from the hole and the men, communing with himself and still amazed that things should have come to this. It was hard to believe that scarcely two weeks ago he had taken command of the U-boat for a special mission with no inkling whatever of the disaster it would turn out to be. Yet how could he have foreseen anything so bizarre? And in his ignorance of the plotting that was going on, how could he have acted to avoid the consequences? He had done nothing wrong, and yet he was to be punished. There was no justice in it.

And then he remembered what Spranger had said: 'You still have the choice. You could still throw in your lot with us.'

So why not do just that? Why be a martyr? How would his death be of any benefit to his country or his Party? Even to the Führer. It would accomplish nothing. It would be a useless, foolish gesture, nothing more.

He came to a halt, turned, walked back to the group of men. He saw that the digging had been completed and that the first of the boxes was being placed in the hole.

He spoke to Spranger: 'I have changed my mind. I wish to join you.'

They all stopped working and stared at him. For a moment or two there was dead silence except for the murmur of the surf in the background.

Then Spranger said: 'You have left it a little late.'

'But not too late, I hope.'

'You genuinely wish now to be part of the operation? To stick with us in Brazil and later?'

'Yes.'

A man said contemptuously: 'He just wants to save his skin, that's what.'

'And what if he does?' Spranger said. 'Isn't it natural? Wouldn't you in his situation?'

'Yes, but can we trust him?' It was Petty Officer Georg Borchert who was speaking now. 'Suppose we take him with us, and as soon as he gets to Brazil he turns on us and does every damn thing to make trouble. Like he could, you know.'

'In what way?'

'Well, like going to the German Embassy in Rio or wherever and telling the tale. Then they could maybe make it hot for us by using their influence with the Brazilian government to arrest us or some-thing.'

'Question is,' Spranger said, 'does the German Embassy have any influence left with the Brazilians? They could be more inclined to back the other side from what I've heard.'

'Me, I wouldn't take the risk.'

Then everybody started talking at once, and it was plain to see that there was little support for the idea of admitting Hartmann to the exclusive circle of the mutineers. None of them had ever liked him, and now they did not trust him.

Hartmann had to raise his voice in order to be heard above the babble. 'I promise you I will do nothing to make trouble for you. I do not even ask for a share of the gold.'

'Well,' Borchert sneered, 'that's very generous of you, seeing as you haven't done a thing to help get it. If you'd had your way it would still be heading for Argentina. You wouldn't believe it was just going to be banked there for some top bastard of a Nazi, ready for when he decided to cut and run. So have you changed your mind about that?'

'I think I may have been wrong,' Hartmann admitted.

'And I say it's not good enough. I say we'd be mad to take you along with us.'

'So you intend to leave me here to die?'

'People have had worse things done to them.'

Hartmann appealed to Spranger, as though seeing in him someone who would give him a sympathetic hearing. 'If I were to give you my sworn word not to do anything to harm any of you. My word as a man of honour. What then?'

One of the seamen standing close to him said: 'You, a man of honour! Why, you're nothing but a gottam Nazi bastard. I spit on you.'

And he did so. The spittle hit Hartmann in the face and ran down to his chin.

It was too much to be tolerated, too deep an insult. Hartmann could not restrain himself. He slapped the man hard on the cheek.

'Animal!'

The man, who was a heavily built six-footer, retaliated with a fist to the chin. It was delivered with all the weight of the man, and it sent Hartmann down. He fell flat on his back, and in falling the base of his skull struck the edge of one of the boxes that were waiting to be buried. The crack of the impact was audible to all of them. It sounded like a stick being snapped in two, but it was in fact the bone breaking.

Hartmann did not get up.

They did not realize at first that he was dead, but it soon became apparent that he was. The man who had struck the blow began to excuse himself.

'He asked for it. He shouldn't have hit me. It was his own fault. You can't blame me.'

But in fact no one was blaming him. He had in effect solved a problem for them. They no longer had to decide whether or not to accept Hartmann's word that he had had a genuine change of heart and that if they took him with them he would do nothing to betray their trust.

'Well,' Spranger said, 'now we've got to leave him here.' And he felt relieved that the problem of what to do with the captain had been solved in this way. 'Now let's get on with burying the gold.'

There remained the question of what to do with Hartmann's body. Left in the open to rot, it might be discovered by some chance visitor to the island; and though that in itself would not reveal the hoard of gold, questions might be asked and the island might come under scrutiny. It would be best, therefore, to bury the body; and where better to do that than on top of the gold? In a macabre sort of way Hartmann might be regarded as a guardian of the treasure.

He put the idea to the others, and it was agreed.

Then one of the men said that dead men had no need of shoes, and he could use Hartmann's. So he took them. And then another man took the shirt, and a third took the shorts. Hartmann was now naked and all his dignity had gone. Müller for one did not approve of this stripping of the body; he thought it was degrading and should not have been done. But he said nothing.

When the remaining boxes had been lowered into the hole, the body was laid on top of them. When digging the hole they had had no notion that anything would be buried with the gold, and they had left little room above the boxes. As a result, only a thin layer of sand covered the corpse when they had finished the job. They could have piled more sand in a mound, but they decided not to do this, since it might attract attention if anyone else came to the island. Instead, they scattered the excess of sand and left no marker to indicate where the grave was. Spranger made a note of its position in relation to two of the trees, which he marked with knife-cuts, and was sure that he would be able to locate it again when they returned. He hoped this would not be very far into the future.

The tide had turned when the job was finished and they had returned to the U-boat. A few more hours and the bows were lifting from the sand. The engines were started and put into reverse, and with no trouble at all the boat was hauled into deeper water.

It was almost dark when they left the bay and headed out to sea, leaving behind them a treasure in gold bullion and the corpse of Captain Klaus Hartmann to guard it.

15

Lucky Man

THEY set course for Rio de Janeiro, sailing for the most part on the surface. There was a relaxed feeling on board; everyone was aware of it. It was as though already they felt that for them the war was over and that for the present they had no more to do than proceed on this last voyage to Brazil and give themselves up. There they would stay until the end of that madness they had left behind in Europe was finished and then return to the island where their treasure lay buried.

It was a sweet vision, and perhaps they had allowed themselves to be so dazzled by it that they failed to stay as alert as they should have been to the danger that still threatened them where they were.

It was on a fateful afternoon, possibly a hundred miles to the east of the Lesser Antilles when a Royal Navy destroyer came up over the horizon unobserved by the drowsy lookout or officer of the watch in the conning-tower. It was firing at them with its 4.7 inch guns before anyone was aware that it was there.

Müller had ben basking in the sun on the afterdeck, half-asleep, when he was brought fully to his senses by the sound of gunfire. He saw a spout of water where a shell had fallen short of the target on the starboard side; and then he was on his feet and running for the conning-tower, together with three other seamen who had been in the sunbathing company. In the mad scramble one of his companions barged into him and sent him flying overboard on the port side.

He went under and the U-boat slid past him, almost catching him with the churning propeller. Then it was gone and he came to the surface yards astern of it. He saw a shell strike the conning-tower while some of the men were still trying to climb into it. He heard screaming.

He swam away from the U-boat. For a long time it had been his home, but he had never loved it. He knew he would never go back to it now. He heard the screech of another shell, and when he stopped swimming and looked back he saw the stern of the U-boat sticking up almost vertically above the water, while the conning-tower and the forepart had disappeared. He began swimming again, and when he looked back a second time the U-boat had vanished completely.

So it had gone, that iron tube like a monstrous cigar, and though he had hated it, now that it was no longer there, he felt the loss. He felt too an awful loneliness; so small an island of human flesh in that vast mass of salty water. Wretched though life on board the U-boat had been, at least there had been companionship within those metal walls. Now all that was gone and he was alone.

Now and then he caught sight of the destroyer, still some distance away but coming closer. He wondered whether it would drop depth-charges where the U-boat had gone down; and he wondered whether he was far enough away from the spot to be safe from the explosions. He tried desperately to put more distance between himself and that possibly lethal place, but he had never been a strong swimmer and he quickly tired.

He came to a floating carpet of oil, and he knew that he had lost direction and had maybe been swimming in a circle which had brought him back to the point from which he had started. He tried to get away from the oil, but a lot of it clung to him and it was a while before he could manage to get away from the patch and into clear water.

He was really tiring now, and the taste of the salt and the oil was in his mouth. He felt that it was pointless to struggle any longer. He was finished; that was the truth of it. And then he thought of all that gold which none of them would ever get their hands on after all. It was Hartmann's now, the lot of it. He was lying on it and no one would take it from him. But much good it would do him: a dead man.

So this was the end of it, the end of that dream of great wealth and easy living. Like all dreams, it had melted away, ephemeral as a wisp of cirrus cloud in the blue summer sky.

He had given up hope when they picked him up. He did not know until later that they had been searching for survivors and had found none but him. He was so exhausted they had to help him up the Jacob's ladder. He was smeared with oil and there was salt on his tongue. He felt like death but knew he was alive.

They cleaned him up and took him to the sick bay and ran the rule over him and said he would be all right. Müller knew enough English to understand what was said to him if it was spoken slowly and clearly. He was told he was lucky to be alive, seeing that no one else had survived the sinking of the U-boat. He really was one very lucky man.

It was quite a while before it dawned on him that he was now the only person in the whole wide world who knew where the Nazi gold was buried. He was a rich man if only he could manage to pick up his wealth.

He did not tell anyone this.

It was his secret.

16

No Hoax

When Müller was repatriated he had nothing to go back to in Germany: no family, no home, no job. He went back to a defeated country of shattered buildings and soup kitchens and armies of occupation. The leaders of Nazi Germany were on trial in Nuremberg for crimes against humanity, and the Russians were systematically dismantling factories in their zone and transporting the machinery to their own country.

Müller, fortunately, had no contact with the Russians. He was in the British zone, the north-west portion of the country. He returned initially to the small town where he had worked before the war; but it was a pile of rubble, and even the survivors amongst those people he had known in those days were like strangers to him now.

He did not stay long. There was nothing for him in that place. It was his past, and he had to look to the future, which was golden, if only he could find a way of getting the gold.

That was the difficulty. Somehow he had to return to that island in the Bahamas where the boxes lay buried, and dig them up and carry them away. The first thing of course that was needed was a boat, a seagoing yacht. And he had no money to buy one. And even if he somehow obtained the money and bought the boat, he would need to sail it single-handedly across the Atlantic. He had never sailed a boat in his life, and his U-boat service in the German Navy had not made him a sailor. So that was something he would need to learn; which would take time and more money. He had the time but not the cash.

After much thought and much heart-searching he was driven to one inescapable conclusion: he would have to take a partner. He did not like it; any sharing of the treasure was anathema to him; he regarded it as his by right, and his alone. But what was the use of a treasure, however large, if it was unobtainable? How would it profit him buried in that faraway hole in the sand under the corpse of Captain Klaus Hartmann? Better to forfeit a part than lose it all. Half a loaf was certainly better than no bread; especially when the bread was golden.

He drifted north to Hamburg with the vague idea that in a great seaport he might find the partner he needed. Hamburg had been devastated by high-explosive and raging fire. Wave after wave of heavy aircraft had crossed the North Sea by night and poured down upon it a deadly rain of bomb and incendiary. Seen from the air it had been one great bonfire in which the glitter of each new explosion had been visible to the air-crews gazing down from their Lancasters and Halifaxes.

Müller had gone to Hamburg hoping that he might fall in with someone who could help him with his problem. In dockland cafés and bars where seamen tended to congregate he started conversations with perfect strangers in order to introduce the subject of long-distance sailing in small boats, of treasure-hunting and such matters. But he could see that it was useless, for these men were deckhands from cargo vessels, stewards from passenger liners, or just dockers who had never been to sea in their lives.

And even if they had been pukka yachtsmen with boats of their own, which was unlikely to say the least, they would never have guessed from the vague and guarded manner in which he introduced the subject that what he was talking about was real treasure buried on a real desert island far across the ocean. Nor would they have realized that it was this same ocean that was the snag, the almighty snag that prevented him from getting his hands on ninety-eight bars of solid gold.

Moreover, even if he had told them there was indeed a cache of gold, and that it was just waiting for him to dig it up if only he could find a way of getting to it, would they have believed him? Not likely. They would have thought he was spinning a yarn and would have put him down as a bit of a crank, harmless but something of a nut-case.

To earn some kind of a living he was working in a very menial way on the restoration of the city. It was unskilled manual work; for, as an ex-clerk in a lawyer's office and an ex-submariner, he had no skills in the building line. But there was plenty of labouring work available, such as clearing rubble, sorting bricks for reuse, pushing wheelbarrows and so on. Power tools and machinery were at a premium, but there was much that could be done with the bare hands, and there were plenty of these available.

Müller lived in a cellar with a lot of other people and not a few rats. It was crowded and it stank, but you had to live somewhere. And all the time he was plagued with the thought of that fortune in gold which he could not reach and which someone else might discover before he could claim it for his own. He told himself over and over again that this was highly improbable, since no marker had been left to indicate where the gold was buried, and maybe nobody visited the island more than once in a blue moon anyway. But none of this reasoning stopped him from worrying.

He saw that he was getting nowhere and time was passing. He could not help thinking of the good life he could enjoy if only he had the gold. He would be so rich that he could leave Germany altogether; go to America perhaps, or Spain, or the French Riviera. He would live a life of ease in the sun, buy a luxury villa, have a choice of attractive women . . . He dreamed of it and awoke to the same old squalid cellar and the miserable hand-to-mouth existence.

He decided to put an advertisement in the agony column of a Hamburg newspaper which was used by people trying to contact relatives or friends with whom they had lost touch in the aftermath of the war and so on. He gave much thought to the wording of his piece and rewrote it several times before coming up with what he considered a satisfactory version. He needed to make it sufficiently attractive to the right sort of person without giving too much away. He certainly could not state precisely what the situation was, but he had somehow to convince the reader that there was something in it – something worth following up.

The entry he finally submitted to the paper ran thus: 'Former U-boat rating seeks yachtsman as partner in treasure-seeking enterprise. This is not a hoax. I know where the treasure is.'

His name was not given. There was a box number to which any replies had to be addressed. Having handed in this item at the newspaper office and paid the fee, he went away to await results.

He waited four days before going back to check whether any replies had come in. There were just five. He had expected more, but he took them away to read, in hope rather than expectation of anything worthwhile being enclosed in the shoddy envelopes.

Four of them he discarded at once. One of them was from a former sailor who apparently thought he already had a yacht and simply wanted someone to make up the crew. Another replied at great length in almost illegible handwriting, outlining a scheme he had for extracting gold from sea-water. All he needed was a small amount of capital to get the enterprise up and running. He was obviously a crank; as were two of the others. Only the fifth letter seemed to hold more promise.

It was better written, and the writer stated that he had been an officer in the German Navy. He did not say what rank he had held, but he said he was most interested in the proposition outlined in the advertisement. He suggested a meeting, so that they could talk things over. He gave an address and said that he looked forward to hearing from the advertiser so that they could arrange a time and place.

His name was Otto Weyland.

17

Not Joking

THEY met in a grubby little café that was no more than a temporary structure thrown together for the most part with salvaged
materials. It was near the docks on the north side of the Elbe and
the clientele was largely made up of dockers and seamen. It was
Müller who had suggested this meeting-place, and there was no
doubt that it was easier for him to get to than it was for Weyland,
whose address was some distance away. The fact that he had made
no objection to Müller's choice of rendezvous suggested that he
was eager for the meeting to take place. Müller took this as a good
sign.

He had given Weyland a brief description of himself, and at the
appointed time he was sitting alone at a small table in a corner with
a cup of ersatz coffee in front of him. He was dressed in rather
threadbare grey trousers and a blue jersey with a knitted woollen
cap on his head. He might easily have passed for a seaman. There
were several other customers in the place, but most of them were
sitting on stools at a long counter. None of them were taking any
notice of him.

After he had been waiting for ten minutes or so and had smoked
a cheap cigarette he began to doubt whether Weyland would turn

up. Perhaps he had never intended to. But that seemed unlikely after he had taken the trouble to reply to the advertisement. Müller had taken only a few sips of the coffee and the rest was now luke-warm. He picked up the cup, drank some more of the rather vile stuff, and heard a voice close to his ear say quietly;

'U one nine five three.'

It startled him, and he spilt some of the coffee. He could not understand how the man who had uttered the words could have come so close without his noticing him. And that number, spoken in little more than a whisper, like an echo from the past!

'Ah!' the man said. 'I see that means something to you. Good.'

Müller set the coffee cup down and looked at him. He was a rather tall and skinny individual, possibly in his middle or late thirties and with a slight stoop. His face put Müller in mind of a bird of prey; there was the beak of a nose and the dark probing eyes that seemed to be boring into him. He had an uneasy feeling that Weyland could read his mind. He also had an idea that he had seen the man somewhere before, though he could not remember where.

'You are Otto Weyland?'

'Yes,' the man said. 'And you, of course, are Heinz Müller. I am happy to meet you.'

He sat down on a chair, facing Müller across the table. He was dressed in a dark grey suit that was old and worn but was of good quality. He was bareheaded, and his lank black hair was receding from the forehead.

Müller was not sure he liked the look of Otto Weyland, but he feared he might be stuck with him now. He looked the sort who might be hard to shake off if he did not wish to be. And it was obvious that he knew something about the U-boat that had been lost in the Atlantic. How much that something was had yet to be disclosed.

'So,' Weyland said, 'what is all this about a treasure?'

Müller answered warily with a question of his own. 'What do you know about U-boat one nine five three?'

Weyland smiled faintly. 'Quite a lot. I know for example what cargo she was carrying on her last ill-fated voyage.'

'How do you know that?'

'I know,' Weyland said, 'because I was at the U-boat base in Brest when it was delivered. I supervised the transfer from the truck that brought it.'

'Ah!' Müller said. And he knew now why he had had that feeling that he had seen the man before.

Both men were talking in low voices, though it was hardly necessary, since no one was paying any attention to them.

'I heard later that the boat had been lost, though there were no details. Later still there was a rumour that she had been sunk by a British destroyer and that there had been only one survivor, picked up by the warship and taken as a prisoner of war to England. I never learnt his name. Now of course I assume that it was Heinz Müller. Am I correct?'

'Would you believe me if I denied it?'

'I should find it difficult to believe.'

Müller's brain was racing, and he sensed that he might be in some danger. Suppose he were to tell Weyland the whole story. Would the man be a stickler for law and order and feel it his duty to report him to the authorities? For there could be no doubt that he, with others now dead, had committed a most serious crime by taking part in a mutiny on the high seas, in the stealing of a load of gold bullion presumably belonging to the German government, and in the killing of the captain of the U-boat, though that had been an accident. But what authorities could he be reported to? The British, who were now occupying this zone? Would they wish to know? Had they not enough to handle already?

Weyland might have been reading his thoughts. He gave a

sardonic grin. 'If you are worried about anything illegal you may have done, forget it. I am interested only in the gold. I fail to see how it can possibly be, but from the wording of your advertisement it would seem that somehow or other the bullion is not at the bottom of the sea but in some place where it is waiting to be picked up. When you referred to a treasure it was the gold you had in mind, wasn't it?'

'Yes,' Müller said. He could see no point in denying it now. Weyland would not have believed him.

'So now perhaps you will tell me the whole story.'

Müller hesitated; then gave a shrug and said: 'Why not?' If he wished to persuade Weyland to help him, there could be no glossing over the details regarding the way in which the gold had come to be buried on the island. 'Get me another cup of coffee and I'll tell you.'

Weyland went to fetch the coffee and came back with two cups. Müller said: 'What do you know about the gold?'

'How do you mean?' Weyland asked.

'I mean do you know where it came from and what the purpose was in sending it to Argentina?'

'The official story was that it was going to pay for munitions for the German army.'

'And do you believe that?'

'No. I think it was being sent there by someone or some group high up in the Party as an insurance against a German defeat. Someone was planning to cut and run, and intended to have money in the bank when the time came.'

'Do you know who it was?'

'No. It would have been a well kept secret. Secret even from the Führer himself. Maybe it was Martin Bormann. He vanished, and there've been reports of his being sighted in South America.'

'But without the gold.'

'True. Was there any feeling on board the U-boat that the operation was not what it seemed?'

'Oh, yes. There were plenty who had doubts. I'd say the only one who didn't have any was Captain Hartmann. Or if he did have doubts he was determined to carry out his orders regardless.'

'Yes, he would be. It was probably why he was put there. And in the end he went down with the boat.'

'No.'

Weyland raised an eyebrow. 'No? You don't mean to tell me he's still alive?'

'No, not alive. In fact it might be said that even in death he's carrying out his duty like a true Nazi guarding the gold.' Müller smiled faintly. 'Very steadfastly.'

'Now you're being very cryptic,' Weyland said. 'Enlighten me please.'

'There was a mutiny. It took place soon after we'd been refuelled by the milch cow. Captain Hartmann was supplanted, and then we altered course and made for the Bahamas. On one of the uninhabited islands the gold was taken ashore and buried.'

'I see. And Hartmann?'

'He had an accident. We buried his body with the gold.'

'So that is how he's guarding it,' Weyland said. 'Can't say I grieve for him. Never liked the man. Too much of the dedicated Nazi. Ex-Hitler Youth. Idolised dear Adolf. Bone from the neck up. I suppose he never weakened?'

'As a matter of fact, he did. We were going to leave him on the island. It must have scared him. He begged to be allowed to join us.'

'And so you killed him?'

'No. I told you. It was an accident. He hit one of the seamen. The man knocked him down and he cracked his skull on one of the boxes.'

'Very convenient.' Weyland spoke sardonically. 'So you buried him with the gold to save the bother of digging another grave.'

'You could put it that way.'

'And after leaving the island, what did you propose doing?'

'To go to Brazil and give ourselves up. After the war we planned to return to the island, dig up the gold and share it out. We took one box for expenses.'

'But of course you never reached Brazil.'

'No. This British destroyer sank us.'

'Leaving you as the sole survivor.'

'Yes.'

Weyland drank some coffee, grimaced and set the cup down. He was silent for a time, as if turning over in his mind what he had just heard. Then he said: 'And now the situation is this. You know where there is a fortune in gold for the taking and you have no way of getting to it. Is that so?'

'Yes. That is why I have to take a partner. Someone with the means to get us to the Bahamas.'

'In short, someone with a yacht and the skill to sail it across the Atlantic.'

'Yes. Do you possess that skill?'

'I do,' Weyland said.

'Ah!' Müller's face brightened.

'But I have no yacht.'

Müller's expression changed to one of despondency. 'Then you cannot help me.'

'Don't be too hasty,' Weyland said. 'I had a yacht before the war. I did a great deal of sailing. Deep sea stuff. I can handle any boat. And I am not simply boasting, I assure you.'

'But you haven't got one now?'

'Sadly, no.'

'What happened to it?'

'God knows. It may not even be afloat now. Even if it were and I had it, there might be complications if we tried to sail from a German port. I don't know what restrictions there are in that respect, but there are bound to be some. It might be better not to start from here.'

Müller thought Weyland was making a joke. And not a very good one. 'Where else could we start from?'

'Denmark,' Weyland said.

And it was evident that he was not joking.

18

The Key

'YOU have not told me yet the name of the island,' Weyland said. 'You do know it, I suppose?'

'Yes, I do know it.'

'But you are not going to tell me?'

'Not yet. It is a secret. But nothing is a secret if more than one person knows it.'

Weyland smiled. 'I see that you are being cautious. But I shall have to know where this island is if I am to navigate a yacht to it.'

'Agreed. But it will be time for that when we are on our way.'

'As you will. I don't blame you. What guarantee would you have that I wouldn't double-cross you and go for the treasure without you?'

'None. But I don't think you would do that. I believe you are a gentleman.'

'Perhaps I am. But there is no von before my name. Possibly it's as well. Ribbentrop has one and he was never a gentleman. Still, if it helps at all, I give you my word that I will deal honestly with you.'

'I do not doubt it.'

'Good. We shall need money of course. Have you any?'

'Very little. And you?'

'I may be able to raise enough for our purpose. It would be ridiculous, wouldn't it, to be denied possession of this great fortune in gold by the lack of a modest amount of ready cash?'

Müller agreed that it would.

'Where are you living?' Weyland asked.

Müller told him.

Weyland said: 'You had better come and live at my place for the present. We need to keep in touch. Does that suit you?'

It suited Müller very well. He had no idea what Weyland's place was like, but it could hardly be worse than the overcrowded cellar.

It turned out to be a big old house on the north side of the city in what had once been a rather classy residential district. There was a large garden, utterly neglected, with trees and shrubs and one or two stone statues and a ruined arbour and a fountain that was not working.

Weyland told Müller that this was the family home. 'My parents and my wife lived here until they were all killed in an air-raid. The irony of it is that they went to an air-raid shelter which took a direct hit; yet if they had stayed here they would have been alive today. The house escaped with very little damage. It has suffered more from its present occupants.

The present occupants were homeless people and their families, who had been allotted rooms in the house and who shared the kitchen and bathrooms. Weyland himself, although the legal owner of the property, had to be content for the present with an attic which had once been occupied by two chambermaids.

'It was,' Weyland said, 'all that was still vacant when I returned home. Others were here before me.'

'But you'll have the whole of the property restored to you eventually, I suppose.'

'Who knows? Perhaps I shall be able to buy something better, eh?' He smiled. 'That would be nice.'

They had reached the attic by way of the backstairs, carpetless and creaking. There were two iron bedsteads in the room, flock mattresses and coarse grey blankets for bedding. A plain deal washstand, a chest of drawers with a swivelling mirror on top, a wardrobe and two rush-seated chairs made up the rest of the furniture.

Müller had brought all his luggage in a kitbag. It did not amount to much. For a man who had hopes of being a millionaire, he was starting from a very low base.

'Now,' Weyland said, 'I shall have to find a telephone that is working. I have some arrangements to make. You can come with me or stay here; whichever you wish.'

Müller decided to go with him. He felt reluctant to let this new partner out of his sight. They had to go some distance to find the telephone, which was in a post office. Weyland used it and then rejoined Müller.

'All right?' Müller asked.

'I'd say so.'

By the time they got back to the house it was growing dusk.

'Now the next thing is to get the merchandise,' Weyland said.

Müller refrained from asking what the merchandise was. He was eager to find out, but he knew that his curiosity would soon be satisfied.

Instead of going into the house, Weyland led the way round to the back and along a path to a walled-in kitchen garden. The wall was crumbling, and the gate giving access through an archway was hanging by a single hinge. Inside some rather half-hearted attempts at cultivation had been made, but for the most part the garden was as neglected as the one outside.

'This way,' Weyland said.

He went ahead along what had once been a gravel path but was now covered with coarse grass and weeds, and Müller followed. They came to a dilapidated greenhouse with most of the glass broken, and went inside. Near the doorway was a spade with a broken handle. Weyland picked it up and walked on, Müller following close behind.

At the far end was a pile of earthenware flower-pots of various sizes, most of them broken. Weyland cleared these to one side and started to dig a hole in the ground beneath the place where they had been. About two or three feet down the spade struck something solid. A little more digging and he had unearthed a rectangular object which he hauled to the surface.

It was now almost dark, but Müller could just discern that what had been drawn to the surface was a black metal deed box.

'Now it's your turn to do some work,' Weyland said. He handed the spade to Müller. 'Fill it in.'

Müller did so. Then he and Weyland replaced the flower-pots to disguise all evidence of digging.

'Though,' Weyland said, 'it's hardly necessary now. I don't think this box will ever be going in there again.'

They left the kitchen garden and made their way back to the house, Weyland carrying the black box under his arm. They went up the unlighted backstairs and into the attic room. Weyland flicked a switch to see whether there was any electricity coming through. There was, though the voltage must have been low, for the one small bulb in the ceiling gave only a dim yellowy light.

He put the deed box, which was dirty and somewhat rusty in places, on the chest of drawers.

'Now,' he said, 'let's see what we have here.'

Müller guessed that he himself knew very well what was in the box and that the words were just uttered for effect. But when Weyland had levered up the lid with a knife the contents were certainly a surprise to Müller. Under a covering of blue velvet and nestling in a bed of the same material was a collection of jewellery which sparkled as if with internal fire even in the weak light of the one small electric bulb.

'My dear parents had the foresight to bury this little nest egg,' Weyland said. 'And also to tell me where it was hidden. Can they have had a foreboding of what was to come?'

He picked up a necklace and let it dangle from his fingers. 'Diamonds. I remember her wearing this when I was a child.'

'It is beautiful,' Müller said. He had never been closer to such an object than a jeweller's shop window.

'As she herself was. My wife too; my wife too.' A note of regret and of hopeless longing had crept into Weyland's voice.

Müller could tell that he was remembering; that the jewels had brought the memories flooding back and the bitterness of irretrievable loss. Müller, who had never had a wife, could understand and sympathize. He had been in love too. He too had suffered a bereavement.

Weyland replaced the necklace and fingered other pieces in the box: rings, bracelets, earrings, brooches . . .

'I have to confess that I have already sold some of the jewellery. It has been necessary. One must live.'

'And now you are planning to sell all the rest?'

'Again it is necessary. We shall need all the money we can get for them. It will be far below the true value of course, but that has to be accepted. These are not normal times.'

'That is certainly true.'

'You would like to come with me when I make the sale?'

'Yes.'

Weyland smiled. 'You really intend to keep an eye on me now that we are partners, don't you?'

'Does it surprise you?'

'No,' Weyland said, 'it doesn't surprise me. But I am hardly likely to run away. You still hold the key to the gold. The name of the island.'

'That is true,' Müller said.

19

Dollars

A FEW hours later they were standing on a piece of waste ground in the shadow of a burnt-out factory. There was no light other than that of the moon, which was near the full but obscured by thin cloud. There was a road some fifty yards away, but not much traffic on it at that time of night. A rough track, once paved, led from the road to where they were standing.

'You're sure your man will come?' Müller asked. He was shivering a little, partly from nervousness and partly from the cold.

There was a chill in the air; a threat of rain.

'I am sure of nothing,' Weyland said. 'This is an uncertain world. All I can say is, he's been reliable in the past. After all, it's to his advantage as well as ours.'

'You've done much dealing with him?'

'No, not much. Some.'

He was carrying the jewels in a pocket of his jacket. They made a bulge against his right hip.

Müller wondered what the factory had produced before being put out of action by heavy bombing and the fires that followed. He had never seen the ruins in daylight, but Weyland knew the place. He had done business there before.

A few more vehicles went past on the road, headlights probing the gloom. Then one slowed and made a turn on to the track leading to the derelict building. It came to a stop just a few yards from where they were standing and the headlights were switched off. Müller could see that it was a British army utility van of the kind he had seen often enough on the streets of Hamburg. The door on the driver's side opened and a man stepped out. He was wearing battledress and a beret. He looked in their direction, and in a voice that sounded as though it was accustomed to giving orders barked:

'Well, let's have you.'

They walked over to the van, and Müller could make out the sergeant's stripes on the man's sleeves. Weyland had already told him that this was Quartermaster Sergeant Harris of the British Army.

'So it's two of you this time,' Harris said. 'Who's the other bloke?'

'His name is Müller,' Weyland said. 'He is a friend.'

It was the first time Müller had heard him speaking English. He appeared to have no difficulty with the language.

'A friend, is he?' Harris said; and he sounded a trifle suspicious. 'Well, Mr Müller, what have you got to sell?'

'Nothing,' Müller said. 'I'm just company.'

'Company, is it? Well, don't try any tricks, that's all. 'Cause I got this here, see?' He patted the butt of a revolver in a webbing holster on his left side. 'And it's loaded.'

Müller assured him that he had no intention of trying any tricks. It was not what he was there for.

'Right then. Let's have a butcher's at what you got this time, Mr Weyland.'

Weyland took the diamond necklace out of his pocket and handed it to Harris. 'This for a start.'

Harris got back into the van and examined the diamonds with a jeweller's eyeglass under the interior light.

'Have no fear,' Weyland said. 'They're genuine.'

Harris grunted. He was a big coarse-featured man, with a military moustache.

'So what's next?'

One by one he examined the pieces as Weyland handed them to him. When there were no more he said:

'That the lot?'

'Yes,' Weyland said. 'That is all. What will you pay for them?'

Harris scratched his chin, sucked in his cheeks, and finally made an offer.

'Five hundred dollars.'

'You're joking.'

'I never joke about money.'

'But five hundred! Those jewels are worth far more.'

'Not to me, they ain't. I gotta sell them on. I gotta make my profit. I don't play this game for fun.'

'Well, it's too low anyway.'

'So what kinda figure did you have in mind?'

'Fifteen hundred at least.'

Harris laughed jeeringly. 'You'll be lucky, mate.'

Müller listened as the haggling went on. He could see that the sergeant was a hard man to deal with. He was the one with the money and he knew that the seller had to sell; so the aces were all in his hand. Weyland managed to push the offer up to eight hundred, but that was the limit and he had to accept it.

Harris counted out the money in ten-dollar bills and handed them to Weyland. 'Nice doing business with you.'

He wasted no more time, but started the engine, turned the van and drove away. Müller and Weyland watched it go. They saw it get to within maybe a dozen yards of the end of the track when a two-ton lorry appeared at the junction, swung off the road and rammed the van head-on. Both vehicles came to an abrupt stop, and Harris could be seen to step out of the van and tug his revolver out of the holster. He had no time to use it, however, because a man had jumped out of the cab of the lorry with a submachine-gun in his hands, and while Harris was still fumbling with the revolver the gun chattered and put him as full of holes as a colander. He went down and was never likely to get up again under his own steam.

The man with the submachine-gun put the weapon down and began a quick search of the soldier's pockets, and it seemed to Weyland and Müller that he had soon found the jewels, which he immediately transferred to his own pocket. A bit more search turned up a wallet; no doubt the one from which Harris had counted out the dollars. There were probably more of them left in it.

'Let's go,' Müller said, tugging at Weyland's sleeve. He felt that they ought already to have been well on their way. It was not a healthy spot to linger in. 'Let's go.'

The gunman was now looking in their direction. In the shadow where they were standing he had perhaps not noticed them before; but the driver was leaning out of the cab and pointing at them and shouting. It seemed to give the man who had shot Harris the idea of doing the same service for them. He was certainly picking up the submachine-gun, and this looked ominous.

Müller and Weyland decided not to wait and see if he did indeed intend giving a repeat performance; it seemed only too probable. So they started to run; and they had gone scarcely ten yards when all doubts were removed by the chatter of the gun and the whine of bullets passing all too close for comfort.

Fortunately, the corner of the ruined building was not far away, and they went round it like a pair of startled rabbits and kept going. They were soon in among a lot of fallen masonry, and the rubble underfoot made the going hazardous; it would have been possible to get a sprained ankle with no trouble at all. But this applied equally to the pursuer if he was pursuing and had not given up the chase, or indeed had not even started it.

So to make sure they stopped and listened. And they could neither hear nor see anything of him. Which was highly encouraging to say the least. And then they heard the lorry starting up and rumbling away, and they began to breathe more freely.

'They're gone,' Weyland said. 'They just couldn't be bothered with us.'

'There are times,' Müller said, 'when it's really nice to feel unwanted.'

'So let's go back and take a look at the sergeant.'

They returned warily, just in case the gunman had stayed behind. But the caution was unnecessary; he was nowhere around. Only Harris was there, lying where he had fallen, bloodstained and motionless. There was no need to feel his pulse; it had stopped beating a while back.

'What do we do with him?' Müller asked.

'Nothing,' Weyland said. 'The sooner we leave him here and get to hell out of it, the better. We don't want to be involved.'

Müller could see the sense in that, and they got themselves on to the road and started walking at a good brisk pace.

After a while Müller said: 'Who were they?'

'At a guess,' Weyland said, 'I'd say gangsters, black marketeers, scum of that sort. Maybe Harris has been muscling in on their territory and they don't like it. I imagine they'd been trailing him, spotted the van and seized their chance.'

'There'll be trouble over this.'

'No doubt. But we won't be in it.'

Müller lapsed into silence again; but a few minutes later he said: 'Why dollars?'

'Because it's the best currency there is. You can use it anywhere; it's the favourite on the black market. Pounds sterling are next best, but marks are rubbish. Though I have heard it's likely the Deutschmark may be revalued; forty old for one new. The Russians won't like it, but to hell with them.'

'It must be hell anyway in their zone.'

'Very much so. We're lucky to be where we are.'

'And going to be luckier still.'

That day was coming closer now. The first step had been taken. Tomorrow they would take the next one. They were on their way.

20

Crazy Proposal

THEY went by train to Flensburg early the next day. From there they travelled by bus to a small town called Glücksburg farther east. They could have tried to cross the border into Denmark openly, but Weyland was sure they would have trouble that way.

'There was a time not long ago when any German could have walked into that country by right. Right of conquest. It's not like that now. Things have changed. I don't think the Danes care much for Germans.'

'I fear,' Müller said, 'we are not the most popular nation in the world right now. Though I must say I got on quite well with the English while I was over there. Did I tell you I worked on a farm?'

'No.'

'Well, I did. It was just a small place. The farmer's name was Wilson. I used to work for him by day and go back to the prisoner of war camp for the night. I was one of those they trusted, you see.'

'I can understand that,' Weyland said.

From Glücksburg they made their way to a small fishing village on the east coast. There they found a man named Bohl who was willing, at a price, to take them out to sea in his boat and put them ashore on the coast of Denmark some ten miles to the north. The operation was to take place after dark, and the fee eventually agreed upon for this service was forty dollars.

It was a fine night and the sea calm. One thing that worried Müller was the possibility that the engine in Bohl's boat might break down. It was certainly an old one, like the boat itself, and had probably given much service in its time. Now and then it would give a kind of hiccup, and he thought it might stop altogether, leaving them adrift in the Baltic Sea. But it always picked up again, and Bohl appeared to be unworried, so perhaps this was normal behaviour. Müller was also bothered by doubts regarding Bohl's navigational skill, but he supposed the man had had enough experience of this part of the coast to find his way without trouble. There were lights along the shore to give him his bearings and he did not have far to go. Anyway, they were in his hands for the present and had to put their trust in him.

And in the end it all turned out well. They waded ashore on a moonlit beach, carrying their packs, and before they had reached the tidemark Bohl had his boat moving away. During the entire trip he had scarcely spoken, but he had done the job for which he had been paid, and that was all that mattered.

'Now,' Weyland said, 'what we need is to find a road.'

It was well, Müller had to admit, that Weyland spoke perfect Danish. This was hardly surprising, since he had spent much of his youth in Denmark. His mother had in fact been Danish, and this was how he came to have a cousin named Sven Andersen. As a boy Weyland spent long holidays with the Andersens, and Sven and he had been close friends. Sven's father, Knut, had a boatyard at a place called Skeeling, which was just a few miles from the port of Esbjerg on the western side of Jutland. On the day after they had stepped ashore on Danish soil Weyland and Müller arrived at Skeeling.

They were not unexpected. Weyland had telephoned earlier in the day to say that he would be coming with a friend. It was Freya, Sven's wife, who took the call. She said they would all be delighted to see Otto after such a long time, and of course any friend of his would be welcome at the Andersen house. Müller hoped this was true, but he had doubts.

'A stranger, and a German! It is hardly likely they'll be happy to have me in the house.'

'I am a German too,' Weyland said.

'Yes, but you are a near relation. They've known you since you were a boy.'

'Don't worry. They're nice people. You'll like them.'

'Ah, but will they like me?'

'Sure they will. It's lucky you speak English. It's a second language to them.'

Müller thought it might take more than a common language to ingratiate him with the Andersens, but it was the only way forward. They were essential to the plan.

The Andersen house was a large timber building adjoining the boatyard. Weyland had told Müller that the business had been a very thriving one before the war, but he feared it had suffered under the occupation. However, from what he had gathered from correspondence with Sven. it seemed that things were beginning to improve. British and American tourists had started coming again, though not yet in very great numbers.

'I just hope there'll be a boat we can use.'

'You didn't mention that was the purpose of our visit?'

'Not on the telephone. Time for that later.'

The family were all at the house to greet them: Sven and Freya and their eight-year-old twins, Henrik and Margrette, and Knut, who was a widower. If any of them thought it strange that Weyland should have a friend like Heinz Müller, they were far too polite to give any sign of it.

Sven was slightly younger than Otto, and there was little in their appearance to indicate that they were cousins. In contrast to Weyland's black hair and balding forehead, Sven had plenty of wiry fair hair and rather craggy features. He was like a younger version of his father. Freya was a blonde beauty. Müller was captivated by her and envied Sven. The twins were excited to see their uncle, but were a little shy of Müller.

Müller himself felt shy and awkward, all too conscious of the wretchedness of his clothing and the fact that he had not shaved for two days. That Weyland was in little better shape was small consolation. He did not seem out of place in this house.

At the evening meal, when they were all gathered round the large dining-table, Müller felt even more uncomfortable. Weyland and the Andersens would chatter away in Danish, which he could not understand, until one of them would draw attention to the fact that he was being left out, and they would switch to English. But then it was difficult to find anything to say. So many subjects were taboo. The war still hung heavily over them; the bitter memories had not yet been completely banished and maybe never would be. The ghost of Adolf Hitler was there in the background like Banquo's at Macbeth's feast.

He felt an urge to stand up and proclaim: 'I was never a Nazi. I hated the Party.' But it would have been ridiculous and would only have made things worse. So he said nothing.

It was not until later, when the twins had been packed off to bed, that Weyland mentioned the true reason for their visit. Even then he did not reveal the whole of it, but merely stated that he and

Müller planned to make a voyage across the Atlantic in a sailing-boat.

'Why?' Sven asked.

'Oh, various reasons. It would be a challenge, and it would take us away from Germany for a while. Living there at this time is not pleasant. And there are always the memories, you understand.'

Müller wondered whether the Andersens were swallowing this story. It sounded rather thin to him. But some reason had to be given for the proposed voyage.

Knut went straight to the heart of the matter. 'What you are saying is that you need a yacht and you think we may be able to supply it. Is that it?'

Weyland looked slightly embarrassed. This blunt but essentially accurate statement regarding the situation could not be refuted. And it was now revealed that his object in making this journey to Denmark had not been simply to pay a call on his Danish relations. There had been an ulterior motive which had now been brought into the open and could not be denied.

'Well, yes,' he said, 'it did occur to me that you might have something suitable we might hire.'

Sven said: 'We don't usually hire out our boats for voyages of that length. In fact we have never done so.'

'But is there any reason why you should not? We would pay of course.' He did not say that their capital was limited to a few hundred dollars.

'It is not that,' Knut said. But he did not say what it was.

Müller guessed that he might be thinking that it was a crazy proposal, and that if he agreed to it and provided a boat, he might never see that boat again. This, of course, was quite a possibility, and Müller himself, had he not been impelled by the prospect of a fortune waiting to be picked up, would have hesitated to embark on such a voyage.

They talked the matter over for quite a while, and Müller got the impression that though Knut was strongly opposed to the idea, it had a certain appeal for Sven. It might have been the kind of venture he himself would have liked to take part in.

Nothing was settled that evening, but it was agreed that in the morning Sven would show the guests what boats were in fact available. No commitment had been made, and Müller was rather despondent. He was doubtful whether there would be any satisfactory outcome from this journey into Denmark. It might well turn out to be a complete waste of time.

21

Extra Hand

THE tour of the boatyard next morning told them one thing for certain: there was only one yacht that was really suitable for a long ocean voyage. This was a two-masted boat, ketch-rigged and some thirty-five feet in length. It was not new, having been built several years before the war, but it had just had a complete overhaul and was in splendid condition. It was lying alongside a small jetty, and one of the boatyard employees was putting some finishing touches to the interior.

Weyland said he liked the look of her; he liked the look of her very much. Müller was not an expert, having never sailed a yacht in his life, but he liked the look of her too.

'Well, of course,' Sven said, 'if you're aiming to sail across the Atlantic, this is the one. Trouble is, I don't think the old man will let you have her. He thinks you're both mad and that he'd never see you or the yacht again.'

'And you?' Weyland said. 'What do you think?'

Sven laughed. 'I think you're mad too. But I'd like to go with you.'

'You would?'

'Why, yes. It'd be an adventure; something worth doing. Could be the old Viking blood in me stirring.' He gave a sigh. 'Pity it's not on.'

'Perhaps it could be.' Weyland spoke thoughtfully, and Müller glanced quickly at him, wondering what he had in mind. 'Perhaps it just could be.'

'No.' Sven spoke with conviction. 'He's adamant. He's made up his mind about this. I can tell you now that he's decided not to let you have a boat; either this or any other.'

'He told you that?'

'Yes.'

'Don't you have any voice in the matter?'

'Oh, I have a voice, but when it comes to the point he's the one who makes the final decision. He's still the boss.'

'So we've come here for nothing,' Müller said to Weyland when they were alone together. 'All that trouble to get here, and now it's not a bit of use to us. We're as far from getting the gold as ever we were.'

He spoke bitterly. In his heart he was blaming Weyland for bringing him on a wild-goose chase. Weyland had been so confident that he could get a boat from the Andersens, these precious Danish relations of his, and now it had come to nothing. Now they would just have to go back to Germany empty-handed.

But Weyland was not so ready to give up. 'There could be a way.'

'A way of what?'

'Of persuading my uncle to give his approval. You may not like it, of course.'

'Try me.'

'We could bring the Andersens in on the venture.'

He had been right about Müller's not liking it. Indeed, he hated it. It had been bad enough having to share the treasure fifty-fifty with Weyland. Now the suggestion seemed to be that he was to relinquish his grip on even more of it.

'Are you seriously proposing to let them have a share of the gold?'

'If it's the only way of getting the boat, it might be well worth it.'

'No,' Müller said. 'Never.'

Weyland was patient. It was only natural that Müller should object. He could see his treasure gradually being whittled away, and it stuck in his craw. But he would surely come round to the view that this proposal was the only feasible solution to the problem.

'Look at it this way, Heinz. Where else can we go for a boat? We're so pushed for cash that we could hardly afford the necessary stores, let alone the hire of a yacht. And there's another thing: I think it wouldn't take much to persuade Sven to come with us. It would be a great help to have another competent sailor with us.'

'So you don't think I'm competent?'

'I didn't say that. But you haven't had any experience of sailing-boats, have you?'

'I could soon learn.'

'Maybe so. But a third hand would be worth having. And anyway, it would be better to have a smaller share of the gold than none at all. There'd still be plenty. Think about it.'

Müller thought about it. After a while he said rather sulkily: 'What kind of a split are you proposing?'

'Twenty-four bars to them. Thirty-seven to each of us. How does that sound to you?'

'I think it would be giving them too much. What have they done for it?'

'Nothing yet. But they'll be providing the yacht, and maybe provisions and gear for us – oilskins, sea boots, life-jackets, that sort of thing. And the extra hand.'

'If he comes.'

'He'll come,' Weyland said.

They put it to the Andersens that evening after the twins had gone to bed. It meant bringing three more people in on the secret, which Müller regretted; but having given a lot more thought to the matter, he could see no other way. It would have been hateful to have gone back to Germany with nothing accomplished. His hopes had been raised ever since Weyland had suggested the Danish solution to the problem, and now to have them dashed completely would have been sickening in the extreme.

To say that the Andersens were astounded would have been putting it mildly. And at first they were reluctant to believe they were not being hoaxed; though what the purpose of such a hoax could have been was difficult to imagine. And gradually they became convinced that the information they were being given was the truth, bizarre as it might seem.

If it had been Müller's word alone that vouched for the truth of the account they might not have believed; though that such a story could be a complete fabrication would have seemed unlikely. But Weyland's assurance that he himself had supervised the loading of the gold on board the U-boat, and that it was on record that the same vessel had been sunk in the Atlantic not far from the Bahamas with the loss of all hands except one seemed to lend credence to Müller's tale.

So gradually even the last sceptic, Knut, was convinced.

'You see now,' Weyland said, 'why we need the yacht. It is the only way we can get to the island. We would like Sven to go with us to help with the sailing – if he is willing.'

Sven's eyes sparkled. 'I am willing.'

Freya looked less happy, but said nothing.

Knut said: 'Supposing I agree to provide the yacht and Sven goes with you, what do we get out of the deal?'

Weyland told him.

'And how much would that amount of gold be worth?'

'I don't know. But quite a lot. It's not chicken-feed.'

'It would help the business to get back on its feet,' Sven said. 'We could really use it.'

Knut thought about it for a while and came to a decision.

'Very well.'

As Weyland had done, they wanted to know the name of the island.

'Heinz will not tell us,' Weyland said.

'Why not?' Sven asked.

'It does not need to be told until we are at sea,' Müller said.

Knut laughed. 'I see that you are a careful man, Heinz. You play your cards close to your chest. A wise precaution.'

'Don't you trust us?' Freya asked.

'Why should he?' Knut said. 'Two days ago he'd never set eyes on us.'

Müller felt uncomfortable. He would have liked to tell Freya that there was nothing personal in it. He could have explained to her that he was doing her a service by not putting on her the responsibility of keeping his secret. But perhaps it was better to say nothing.

'Well,' Sven said, 'now that's settled we can start making preparations for sailing. Tomorrow looks like being a busy day.'

22

Marker

IT was six days later when the yacht, which had the same name as
Sven's wife, Freya, cast off from the jetty and set out on the long
voyage to the Bahamas. It had taken that time to make all preparations for departure.

They were seen off by the Andersens and the boatyard workers,
who knew nothing of the true purpose of the voyage. Everyone
was waving and putting on a cheerful face, though for Freya the
parting from Sven had not been the happiest of occasions. The
twins were excited; but they, like the employees, were unaware that
the three men in the yacht had such great expectations regarding
the outcome of the voyage. Only Knut and Freya knew they were
witnessing the start of a treasure hunt, and that if all went well this
small vessel would return laden with a fortune in gold.

It was two days later, when they were in the North Sea on course
for the English Channel, that Müller revealed the name of the
island.

'Dove.'

They scanned the chart, and there it was.

'It seems more real now,' Weyland said. 'Now that it has a name.

Before it was something of a phantom; something it was hard to fully believe in. It was as though we were sailing in search of a myth, a chimera. Now it has become solid; it has bearings. Now we really do know where we're heading.'

Müller, though he did not admit as much, was relieved. There had always been at the back of his mind a faint nagging doubt; a feeling that perhaps his memory might have played him false, and that there was no island named Dove; that the name of that small chunk of land where the gold lay buried might in fact have been something else. Now he was reassured and all was well.

'How long will it take us to get there?'

'Who knows?' Weyland said. 'So much depends on the weather, winds, luck. This isn't like a steamship or a motor vessel, ruling off the miles at a steady rate. With sails you're back to the early days of ocean navigation.'

'But at a guess?'

'Three weeks, a month, maybe more.'

The yacht was handling well; that was in their favour. Müller was learning the skills of sailing, which he had never acquired as a seaman in the German Navy; and for the first time he was enjoying life at sea.

The three men got on well together. For a time Müller had felt rather like the odd man out. The other two were after all linked by ties of blood, even though they were of separate nationalities; but he was an outsider, from a completely different social background. Yet there was nothing in their attitude towards him that would have given any hint of this, and he felt himself being drawn more closely to them than he had been to any of his shipmates on board the U-boat. The three of them were a team; that was it; a team. It made him happy, brought a feeling of warmth to his heart. He no longer felt any regret that he would not be getting all the gold for himself.

*

They sailed south to the Canaries and then westward. The winds were favourable; there had been no storms; nothing had gone wrong. Müller took it as a good omen: all would go well; he felt it in his bones. He had waited a long time to claim his prize; it was years now since he had come to the realisation that he was the one person in the world who knew where the treasure lay. He had been forced to share that knowledge in the end; it had been necessary. But he would still be rich, and that was all that mattered. In the balmy airs of the tropics he listened to the creaking of the masts and the slap of water at the bows, and he watched the dolphins that sometimes kept them company and the flying-fish leaping like spurts of liquid silver from the waves. Lying half-naked in the sun, he dozed and dreamed of the great times to come, as they surely would. There could be no doubt about it now.

It was late one afternoon when the island came in sight, and Müller's heart leaped. As they drew near he recognised the shape of it, remembered the reef away to starboard, the bay, the curving beach, the palm-trees in the background. Nothing had changed since he had seen it last as the U-boat pulled away and set course for Brazil on that last ill-fated voyage.

'This is your island?' Weyland asked. 'You recognize it?'

'Oh yes; this is it. It hasn't changed. I remember it well.'

If he half-closed his eyes he could imagine that gathering beyond the beach, the hole dug with pieces of board, the boxes being lowered in. He could see with his mind's eye Captain Hartmann walking away and then coming back to say that he wanted to join the mutineers after all. Then there had been the argument, the blows exchanged, and Hartmann falling backwards to strike his head on one of the boxes. No one had guessed at first that he was dead; but then some of them had stripped the body. It was a vile thing to do, and he had disapproved of it. But he had lacked the courage to say so: and he himself had helped to shovel sand on the corpse when they buried it on top of the gold.

So long ago. And yet so well remembered.

The bay was as still as a mirror when the yacht moved in. The dropping of the anchor shattered the glass. And then the sails came rattling down and the long outward voyage was at its end.

'When we loaded the gold in Brest,' Weyland said, 'I never imagined it was destined to come to a place like this.'

Andersen gave a laugh. 'I don't suppose you did. Nor that you'd ever set eyes on it again. There's luck for you.'

'Some were not so lucky,' Müller said. But he had not thought about them for a long time. Not until now, when these surroundings brought the memory back. And he did not grieve for them, and had never done so. Among them all there had not been one he could truly have called a friend. So he had not felt the loss. 'But perhaps it was meant to happen this way.'

'So,' Weyland said, 'you believe in fate.'

'When it works in my favour,' Müller said, 'I believe in it implicitly.'

They lost no time in going ashore. They inflated the rubber dinghy and paddled it to the beach. They were wearing shorts and canvas shoes, and they waded through the shallows, dragging the dinghy after them to the dry sand. They had brought with them something which the men who had buried the gold had lacked – a spade. Andersen was carrying it and Müller was leading the way and trying to remember exactly where they had dug the hole on that long past day. He knew that it had been fairly near the trees, but they had left nothing to mark the spot.

'Why didn't you mark it?' Weyland asked.

'Precaution,' Müller said. 'Suppose somebody had landed on the island and spotted the marker. As I recall Lieutenant Spranger took some bearings and made a note of them. But I didn't take much notice, and of course they were lost with the U-boat.'

'So we've got to dig around until we find the place. Could take some time.'

'Not so very long perhaps. I'm sure it's in this area. We'll just have to probe with the spade. The boxes are not in very deep.'

Andersen started probing; stamping the spade in to the length of the blade. He found nothing.

'There's a lump of rock sticking up over here,' Weyland said. 'Are you sure you didn't leave it as a marker?'

'Yes, I am,' Müller said.

'Do you remember this rock?'

'No, I don't, but—'

'Give me the spade, Sven,' Weyland said. 'I'm going to dig here.'

Müller said: 'You won't find anything. There were no rocks where we dug.'

Weyland said nothing. He just took the spade from Andersen and began to dig. Müller was still saying it was a waste of time when Weyland uncovered one of the boxes. He shut up then and just watched the digging.

They were all there – the forty-nine boxes. The odd thing was that one of them had been opened and one of the gold bars was missing.

And then it occurred to Müller that something else was missing too.

'Where's Hartmann?'

'Hartmann?' Andersen said.

'Yes. Captain Hartmann. The one who was knocked down, hit his head on a box and died. He should have been lying on top of those boxes. That's where we left him.'

'Well, one thing is certain,' Weyland said. 'He didn't wake up, dig himself out, take one of the pieces of gold and walk off with it.'

'After filling in the hole and leaving a rock to mark the spot,' Andersen said. 'He'd have had to be a very busy corpse to do that. A tidy one too.'

'I wonder whether he's still around somewhere,' Weyland said. 'Let's look.'

'They made a search and found the skeleton partly hidden in the clump of trees close by. It was a somewhat gruesome sight, and Müller seemed particularly affected by it. The last time he had seen Hartmann the flesh had all been on his bones. Not many people got to see the skeleton of someone they once knew. It could be unnerving.

'So now we know,' Weyland said.

Andersen glanced at him. 'What do we know?'

'That somebody beat us to it.'

'But took only one of the gold bars. Why not all of them?'

'Obviously they meant to come back later. That's why the rock was left as a marker. Question is, how long is it since they found the gold and how long will it be before they come for the rest of it? It's not likely they're going to be content with just the one bar.'

'Well, one thing's certain. They're going to be unlucky.'

'And we'd better get the stuff on board.'

It was almost dark when they ferried the last load from beach to yacht. They made no attempt to fill the hole in, but left it with the heap of sand that had come out of it marking the spot. The rock was now superfluous. Anyone who turned up later could easily see where the gold had been but was no more.

They decided to stay anchored in the bay that night. They celebrated with canned beer and made a lot of calculations regarding the possible value of the treasure. The more they drank, the higher the estimates became. One thing was certain: it was worth one hell of a lot.

'And it's ours,' Müller said. 'It's all ours.'

He had waited a long time for this moment, and it was really sweet now that it had come.

They began to sing. They were all feeling somewhat intoxicated, and it was not just the effect of the beer.

23

Storm

THERE was no ceremony when the yacht *Wanderer* slipped away from her moorings in Longville and headed out to sea. Of the four young people on board, three believed they were going to pick up a fortune in gold bars, while the fourth was confident that when they reached the island that treasure would have vanished. She would have liked to tell Carlson that they were leaving so soon; he could have passed the information on to the Dutchman and given him the warning to get started without delay. But it was likely he would be doing that anyway; and if his boat was as fast as Roy had said it was, it should beat *Wanderer* to the prize hands down.

'You're looking very pensive, Jo,' Pippa said. 'What's on your mind?'

'What do you think would be on my mind? Gold, of course. Isn't that what we've all got on our minds?'

'Oh, sure. But I thought there might be something more on yours.'

'Like what?'

'Well, you tell me.'

'I don't know what you're getting at. There's nothing to tell.'

'Okay,' Pippa said. 'You don't have to bite my head off. I'm sorry I asked.'

But she felt that Jo had been acting more than a little oddly this last day or two. She wondered whether it had anything to do with Roy Carlson. Jo had spent quite some time with him, and maybe it was a fact that the embers of that old fire had burst into flame again. If so, it was not going to please Angus Laurie, and he already seemed to have guessed that something of the sort was going on.

Still, one thing was certain: there would be no more contact between Jo and the man of business for the next few weeks. What happened after that remained to be seen, though after the revelation regarding the gold price things could hardly be the same again. Meanwhile, she had a feeling that there was not going to be quite the old easy companionship in the yacht that there had been in the past. There was a certain tension in the air that had not been there before. Perhaps it was the thought of the gold that was making them all nervy. It was certainly something.

Gradually they drew away from the coast and lost sight of the beaches of Florida, where the people with nothing better to do cooked their bodies in the sun. The island they were heading for was on the eastern fringe of the Bahamas, and after three days of sailing they could tell they were not going to make any better time than they had on the voyage in the opposite direction. That was how it was when you were dependent on the wind for propulsion. You could not order it up at will; and when it chose to come, it could be a lot more than you bargained for.

Those three days had seen no easing of tension in the boat. Rayburn and Pippa were still on the same affectionate terms as ever, but the friction between Jo and Laurie seemed to get worse rather than better.

One day Carlson's name somehow cropped up, and Laurie

remarked bluntly: 'We should have guessed that man was a crook from the start.'

Jo came to his defence at once. 'You don't know he's crooked. You have no proof of that.'

'Proof enough, I should think. He does deals with Blok, doesn't he? And you'd hardly call him an honest upright citizen.'

'Well, we asked him to do a deal for us, didn't we? He was arranging things for our benefit, wasn't he?'

'Our benefit! That's a laugh! He was the one who was going to get rich out of it, not us. But now we know what we know there'll be no more of that. He'll have to look for some other suckers to take for a ride.'

'You're saying all this because you don't like Roy. That's the truth of it, isn't it?'

'I'm not the only one who hasn't got much love for him. Pippa thinks he's a heel.'

Jo shot a furious glance at the other girl. 'You said that?'

'Why, sure,' Pippa answered coolly. 'Everybody knows he is.'

'So why did you back me up in proposing him as the guy to handle our business? You damn well did, you know.'

'Of course I did. But the fact he was a heel didn't mean he wasn't a straight dealer. Now I know different. Now I wouldn't touch him with rubber gloves on.'

Rayburn was on deck when these exchanges were taking place in the saloon, but Pippa made a point of telling him all about it later. He regretted the way this sourness was creeping into relations on board, and he could not help feeling that it was chiefly Jo's fault. Pippa's next words lent support to this impression.

'I think she could be hiding something from us.'

'Such as what?'

'Something to do with Roy. She did spend a fair amount of time with him. And that meeting when she said she was going to get her hair done may not have been pure chance. My guess is, it was arranged the previous day.'

'Even so, it could have been just a personal thing. Picking up that old affair where it left off. That's what's eating Angus. He's as jealous as hell.'

'I know. And of course it may just have been as you say. But there could have been something more. That Roy Carlson is a devious sort of guy.'

'Well, even if there is something in what you say, I don't see what he can do. As long as we've got our hands on the gold, we can call the tune.'

'That's true,' Pippa said.

But she still seemed doubtful.

Soon, however, there was something a great deal more urgent to worry them, and it pushed other matters completely out of their thoughts for the present.

It started with a weather report picked up on the radio. This referred to a hurricane that was building up to the east and might be heading their way.

'But surely,' Laurie said, 'this isn't the hurricane season.'

'It's getting close to it,' Rayburn said. 'This could be the first of them.'

'Does that mean it won't be a bad one?'

'I don't know. Let's just hope it's not.'

The girls looked apprehensive when told the news.

'What do we do?' Pippa asked.

'That's a good question,' Rayburn said. 'We could of course make for the nearest harbour and take shelter. The snag is there isn't a decent one at all close. And even if we got to one, I'm not sure it would be a good place to be if a hurricane struck it.'

Laurie was of the opinion that, since the movements of hurricanes were unpredictable anyway, they might as well stay on their present course and hope for the best. Rayburn was inclined to agree, so that was what they did.

Twenty-four hours later they were too close to the hurricane for comfort, and *Wanderer* was taking a hammering from wind and rain and wave. The girls were terrified and stayed below. Rayburn and Laurie had been in storms before and had confidence in the yacht's ability to ride this one out. They put out a sea-anchor, and with sails furled managed to keep her head to the wind. They felt sure they would pull through if conditions got no worse.

They did get worse.

24

No Answer

IN the event it made little difference that Jo had been unable to let Carlson know that *Wanderer* was scheduled to set sail the next morning. He himself drove out to Longville later that day and saw that the yacht had gone from the jetty. He did not need to be told what her destination was, and he lost no time in passing the information on to Willem Blok.

'Must've slipped away early. I didn't know they were ready. Eager to get their hands on the loot, I guess.'

'Could be. Gold's a powerful incentive.'

'So we'd better be on our way too. Don't want to have them getting in first.'

'No chance,' Blok said.

'Your boat ready to go?'

'Needs fuelling up and stores putting aboard.'

'How long will that take?'

'Should be ready tomorrow if I get things moving pronto.'

'I'll meet you at the marina,' Carlson said. 'Morning?'

'You do that.'

Carlson drove to Miami the next morning and found Blok already at the marina supervising the business of getting his cruiser, *Lucky*

Boy, ready for sea. Jake was with him and the Alsatian dog. Blok looked massive in shorts and a Hawaiian shirt, a big cigar stuck in his mouth.

'So there you are,' he said. 'Began to think you'd decided not to come. Too busy to spare the time.'

'You have to be joking,' Carlson said. 'This is one sea-trip I wouldn't miss for the world. Jake's coming too, is he?'

'Oh, sure. He can do the digging. Good with a spade, ain't you, Jake?'

The hunchback returned no answer to this. He looked as gloomy as usual.

'Not that I've ever seen one in his hand,' Blok said. 'But I guess any one of us would be happy to do a bit of spadework when it's gold we're digging up.'

'Maybe,' Carlson said. But he doubted whether Blok would do any of the manual labour. It had to be work enough for him to carry his own weight around.

The boat was really quite a size. Carlson reflected that the three of them would have a lot more elbow room than the four young people in their elderly yacht. That really was cramped accommodation. He wondered how far they had got by this time. Not far enough to outrun *Lucky Boy*, that was for sure.

'Jo wanted to come with us,' he said.

'Did she now! And I guess, you told her it was just not on.'

'I did. Wouldn't have been at all according to plan.'

Blok laughed. 'Gotta hand it to you, Roy. You know how to get round a dame. What's it you got that I haven't?'

Carlson grinned. 'Charm. That's what it's called. Though, mind you, I had that other thing going for me too.'

'What was that?'

'Greed. On her part. She couldn't resist the promise of extra dollars.'

'Will she get them?'

'Some maybe. Just enough to keep her sweet.'

'Roy,' Blok said, 'you sure are one smart operator.'

'Not as smart as you, Will. Nobody else could be that smart.'

Blok laughed. He liked the compliment.

They left the marina soon after midday, edging the way out from the moorings and leaving the cluster of other boats astern. Anybody watching might have thought they were off on a fishing trip – if they thought about it at all. One thing was sure: they would never have guessed what the big cruiser with its powerful diesel engine was really being used for. Some, knowing the reputation Blok had, might have harboured a suspicion that he was in the drug-running business, but gold was something else again.

Blok himself was at the wheel. Taking the boat to sea was a job he would never trust to either of the other men, though both were capable of doing it if necessary. The Alsatian, Wolf, lay down in the wheelhouse and closed his eyes. He seemed bored by the whole operation. He had been on plenty of sea-trips, and for him one was probably much like another.

'I hope,' Carlson said, 'we'll have the gold and be well away from the island before the other lot arrive.'

'We shall be,' Blok said. 'Don't worry. It will not take long to dig up the gold and bring it aboard. And anyway, what can they do to stop us? I have my Colt and Jake has his gun. I don't suppose they're armed. Would you say they were?'

'I doubt it. The British don't carry guns the way Americans do. Except their army of course.'

'Did you bring one?'

'No. I thought I could well leave that side of things to you and Jake.'

'There won't be any need for shooting,' Blok said. 'We'll be long gone when they get there.'

He picked up the storm warning too. He passed the information on to Carlson and Jake. Carlson asked the question that Pippa had asked Rayburn.

'What do we do?'

'We keep going,' Blok said.

'You don't think we should run for shelter?'

'And give those bastards the chance to nip in ahead of us?' Blok was contemptuous. 'Are you crazy?'

'The storm will catch them too. They may not make it.'

'You scared?' Blok asked.

'I don't believe in taking unnecessary risks.'

'Like I said. Scared.'

Carlson said nothing more.

It was in the air. They could sense it. And the sea was feeling it already, before the wind had reached them. There was a long oily swell, and the boat rolled. Wolf was conscious of it too; he was restless, padding around like the animal that had provided him with his name.

Jake went about his allotted tasks, wearing his usual morose expression. It was difficult to tell whether he was alarmed or not. It was his duty to cook food in the well-appointed galley, and the rolling of the boat made this no easy task.

During the night a wind sprang up and gradually increased in force; but it was not yet more than a strong breeze.

'We'll be there by morning,' Blok said. 'Everything's going to be fine.'

Carlson hoped he was right, but he himself was not so confident. Reports were still coming in concerning the hurricane, and it appeared to be moving roughly in their direction. Blok said that anyway it was best to press ahead the way they were going, and then if they were caught by any part of the storm it was likely to be no more than the fringe, which should not affect them too badly. Carlson reckoned this was just wishful thinking. He noticed that Blok made no move to turn in and get some sleep when he was not at the wheel.

Jake kept them going with a succession of cups of coffee, and Blok smoked one cigar after another. Carlson chain-smoked cigarettes and tried to judge whether the wind was increasing in strength. He listened to the beat of the diesel engine and just hoped it would not fail them. If it did, they would be in real trouble.

There was a moon nearly at the full, but clouds kept scudding across it, making the light intermittent. It was a relief when dawn broke and the sun came up. Blok took a sextant reading and did some calculations at the chart table. He reckoned they were within ten miles of Dove. It required only a small adjustment to the helm to bring them dead on course.

Blok was exultant. He had been vindicated in his decision to keep pressing ahead.

'We'll soon be there now.'

But there could be no doubt that the wind had strengthened and the sea was heaving more. Carlson was not at all happy with the look of things; and even the thought of the gold that would soon be theirs failed to banish the apprehension he felt regarding the storm that might yet overtake them.

Nevertheless, when the island came in sight even he had a feeling of exultation. There it was, that small piece of land which hitherto had been for them no more than a mark on the chart and now had become a reality, solid and unmoving. There was the bay and the beach and the palm-trees in the background. It was their Eldorado.

Yet, as they approached more closely, it became evident that there was something else besides; something they had not expected; something they could hardly believe was there. It was a two-masted yacht anchored in the bay.

Blok swore. 'They got here first. How in hell did they do it?'

Nobody had an answer to that question. It was inexplicable.

25

Boarding Party

WEYLAND, Müller and Andersen had celebrated so freely after having taken the gold on board that they were late in turning in. When they had done so they had slept so well that it was broad daylight when they awoke and there was a stiff breeze rocking the boat. Andersen tuned in to a weather report, and this was the first they had heard about the hurricane. In their eagerness to get to the island and claim the treasure they had rather neglected in the last day or two to keep an eye on the weather, taking for granted that it would remain settled. Now they realised that they had been too optimistic.

'So what do we do?' Weyland said. 'Do we set sail and hope not to be caught in anything really bad or do we stay here until it blows over?'

Müller was in favour of staying. He had taken a look at the sea and had not been happy with what he saw. He was really no sailor in spite of the experience he had had, and the nearness of a piece of land, small though it might be, gave him courage.

Andersen was inclined the other way. He thought the anchorage might prove to be a trap rather than a haven. In his opinion it would be wise to get well away from the land and give themselves sea room. He was a true sailor.

Weyland was a sailor too, but he was undecided.

'So why don't we have a meal and think about it?'

'Let's do that,' Andersen said.

They were still having the meal when Blok's cruiser hove into view. And none of them saw it.

'I don't think it's them,' Carlson said.

He had been looking at the yacht through binoculars.

'What do you mean, it's not them?' Blok said. 'It must be.'

'If it is, they've changed their boat. This one's bigger and doesn't look the same at all.'

'So who in hell is it?'

'How would I know?' He shifted the binoculars to give him a sight of the beach and beyond. 'One thing, though; it looks like they've got the gold. There's a pile of sand up there, and they've even left a spade sticking in it.'

'Have they, by God!'

Carlson lowered the glasses. 'We're too damned late after all.'

'Damned if we are,' Blok said. 'We came for the gold and we're going to have it, come hell or high water.'

'You're talking about violence. I'm not sure I like that.' Carlson sounded nervous. 'We don't know how many there are of them.'

'Well, we'll soon find out.'

Blok was steering the cruiser towards the entrance to the bay. He took it inside and brought it up to the yacht where it lay at anchor. The wind was making such a racket by this time that no one on board realised they were no longer alone until they felt the bump against the side.

'What was that?' Müller said.

The question was answered by a hail from Blok. 'Ahoy there! Anyone at home?'

They crowded out into the cockpit to find another boat alongside, and by this time even made fast to the yacht. Jake, with surprising agility, had jumped across to the bows and secured a line to a cleat. Carlson, rather more laboriously, had done a similar job at the stern. So now only squeaking jute fenders separated the two hulls as the boats rose and fell on the troubled waters of the bay.

'Mind if we come aboard?' Blok asked.

It was the last thing the three wanted. They could not understand how this big cabin cruiser had suddenly appeared alongside. Until the moment when it bumped into them they had had no idea that they were not still the only human beings within miles of the island. Moreover, the arrival of this intruder on the scene at this particular time was most unwelcome.

Weyland said: 'The fact is, we were about to leave. The weather seems to be getting worse.'

'That's true,' Blok said. 'But you could be safer where you are. We have to make the same decision ourselves. Let's put our heads together and try to work out the best course to take.'

Without waiting for an answer, in spite of his heavy build, he climbed over the rails and stepped down into the cockpit of the yacht. Carlson and Jake were already aboard, so that *Freya* now had three uninvited guests in occupation.

'Let's go below,' Blok said. And again without an invitation he went down the companionway into the saloon.

Short of seizing him and throwing him back on to his own boat, which with one so heavily built would have been a sheer impossibility, there was nothing the three yachtsmen could do but follow him. Carlson and Jake came too. The dog, Wolf, had also joined them. He had to be near his master.

'Ah,' Blok said, 'you were having a meal. No matter. Our business will not take long.'

He seated himself on one of the settees and left the others to accommodate themselves as they saw fit.

'What business?' Weyland asked. And he could not keep a note of anger out of his voice. 'I know of no business we can possibly have with you.'

Blok took a cigar from his jacket pocket, bit off the end and lighted it with a match. Wolf sat at his feet, tongue lolling.

'What business, you say. But I think you know. The business of forty-nine boxes of gold bars.'

'I don't know what you're talking about,' Weyland said.

But he did know, and he knew that the fat man knew he did.

Blok said: 'Why waste time with such lies? We have seen the sand you dug out of the hole and the spade you left. You knew you would have no more use for it, having got what you came for.'

'Who are you?' Weyland demanded.

'My name is Blok. Willem Blok. American citizen. Not that names are of any importance. We have, of course, come to take the gold. We expected to have to dig it up, but you have done that job for us. All that remains is to have it transferred from this boat to mine.'

'You must be mad.'

'Not in the least. I notice you are no longer pretending you don't have the gold.'

'Whether we have it or not makes no difference. It stays where it is.'

'There you are wrong, pal. We have the means to enforce our will. Show 'em, Jake.'

The hunchback was standing in the doorway at the foot of the companionway. He was still wearing a black suit, and under the jacket was a shoulder holster. He put a hand inside the jacket and took out a snub-nosed revolver.

'He is a good shot,' Blok said. 'As I am also.'

He took a Colt .32 automatic from his jacket pocket and showed it to them.

'You have no right,' Müller cried in a high-pitched voice. 'You have no right at all. I am Heinz Müller, and I was there when we buried the gold, when we brought it ashore from the U-boat. All the others are dead. I am the only survivor; so it is mine, mine.'

Blok listened with interest, as did Carlson too. It was the answer to the puzzle. Or at least part of the answer. So it was Nazi gold, maybe stolen from the Jews. And this man, calling himself Heinz Müller, had been a U-boat seaman. But of course his claim to the gold was no more valid than any other.

Blok gave a laugh. 'Sorry, Mr Müller, but I just don't go along with your argument. In this game it's winner take all, and you just ain't a winner. And now, gentlemen all, it's time we got moving.'

As if to lend emphasis to this statement, a gust of wind hit the superstructure and there was a grinding noise as the two hulls rubbed against each other, separated only by the fenders. There was a sudden patter of rain.

'It's getting worse,' Carlson said. And he did not sound happy.

'So we better hurry,' Blok said. He looked at Weyland. 'Where's it stowed?'

'You find it,' Weyland said.

Blok got up with surprising speed and hit him with the Colt on the left cheek. The blow staggered Weyland and the blood ran.

'Don't play games with us,' Blok said. 'We ain't got the time. Now tell us where the gold is.'

It was Andersen who told him. He could see no point in not doing so, since it would be found anyway. The fact that these men were armed, or at least two of them were, gave them an over-whelming advantage. There was no way they could be successfully resisted. It seemed obvious now that if these were not in fact the ones who had discovered the cache and taken away the single ingot, they must have been told about it by the real finders. For how else could they have known there was buried treasure on the island? Well, it made no difference now.

'It's in the for'ard stowage.'

He realized now with some bitterness that they should have set sail immediately the gold had been brought on board. The decision to stay the night at anchor in the bay had been a disastrous one. But how could they have foreseen that the cruiser would come and that the men in it would be armed?

'Right,' Blok said. 'I see you're one sensible guy. You know when you're beat. Now we'll get busy on shifting that cargo.'

26

Madness

IT was no easy task. The weather had deteriorated with surprising rapidity, and it was still getting worse. Thick black cloud had crept over the entire sky and rain was teeming down, driven by a wind that was almost of gale force.

Blok was in charge of operations, and he had forced Müller and Andersen and even the injured Weyland to lend a hand, threatening to shoot them if they refused. They had no doubt that he would have been prepared to carry out this threat if necessary, and they saw no point in making martyrs of themselves in a hopeless cause. So, angrily and bitterly, they obeyed his orders.

The surface of the bay, which not many hours previously had been glassy smooth, was now being lashed into powerful waves by the furious wind. Blok had lowered the cruiser's anchor to augment that of the yacht, but it seemed doubtful whether even the two would hold for much longer.

Meanwhile, Weyland and Andersen were fetching up the boxes of gold from the stowage under the supervision of the hunchback, Jake, gun in hand. They would then pass them across to Carlson and Müller on board the cruiser, who would dump them in the saloon. Soon they were all drenched to the skin and finding it difficult to keep their footing on the wet decks and in the blustering wind which was becoming ever stronger.

They needed no goading from Blok to keep at it, for in each of them now was a desire to see the task completed and a feeling that they were all in peril from something elemental over which they had no control.

Blok himself was aware of the danger, but his greed for gold was such that it overrode all other considerations. He could hear the grinding of the one boat against the other and doubted whether the anchors were holding; but he refused to cut and run while there was still one box left on board the yacht.

Carlson, fearful of what might happen, urged him to go. 'For God's sake, Will, leave the rest of it. Let's get away from here while we can.'

Blok snarled at him, told him to get back to work, menaced him with the Colt. Carlson, faced with this more immediate threat to his life, went back to his uneasy partnership with Müller.

And at last the transfer of cargo was completed. Jake climbed back on board the cruiser and began to winch up the anchor. Blok had started the engine and was at the wheel. It only remained for the lines to be cast off and the operation would be completed.

Except for one thing. Müller had not yet returned to the yacht. In the gloom and confusion of the storm, in the scudding rain and overall murk and the screeching of the banshee-like wind, no one had noticed that he was still on board the larger vessel. Indeed, the first to become aware of this was Blok.

To Müller perhaps more than anyone else the loss of the gold was a disaster, a deprivation scarcely to be borne. For it was he, the only survivor of the sunken U-boat, who had for years set his heart on obtaining the buried gold of which only he knew the whereabouts and which he regarded as his own by right. It had hurt him to face the necessity of sharing the treasure, first with Weyland and then with the Andersens; but he had reconciled himself to that, for at least he would have been getting a goodly share. But now it was all being taken from him, and that was too much to bear. He could not and would not bear it.

It might have been said that at that moment Müller was mad. He had been driven mad by this great loss and his hatred for the man whom he regarded as responsible for it; this thief who had stolen what was undoubtedly his; this gross villain of a man whose name was Willem Blok.

In his madness he was hardly aware of how the iron marlinspike came to be in his hand; he just knew that it was there; and he knew for what purpose he had it in his gasp. He clawed his way to the wheelhouse and went inside. Blok did not see him come in, but the Alsatian gave a low growl. Müller ignored it.

He said: 'No!'

Blok heard him then and turned to face him.

Again Müller said: 'No!' And then he added: 'You shall not have it. It is mine.'

He had spoken in German, forgetting that Blok would not understand the words. But this was of no account, since actions spoke louder than words, and Müller's action was to strike Blok on the forehead just between the eyes with the heavy iron marlinspike; and then in rapid succession to strike him again and again, so that the blood spurted and Blok went down, not having uttered a cry.

Even then Müller might have gone on striking him, had not Wolf got up from the floor and made a spring at him. It was the dog's teeth closing on his throat that stopped him; it was the teeth in the jugular letting the life-blood flow that killed him.

Carlson would never have wished to assume command of the cruiser, but with Blok lying bloody and unconscious on the floor of the saloon, to which they had dragged him, there was no alternative. Jake, who had already cut the lines securing the cruiser to the yacht, refused to give any more help. He and Wolf stayed in the saloon to watch over their master, who appeared to be in a coma.

Carlson was appalled and terrified, but he knew that it was essential to get the cruiser out of the death-trap of the bay, where it would almost certainly be driven aground and battered to pieces. He was fearful of the open sea in this storm, but it was the lesser of two evils. So in this extremity he took the helm and got the cruiser heading for the entrance to the bay, the ghastly corpse of Müller lying only a yard or two from his feet and seeming to gaze up at him in mute disapproval.

In the murk it was difficult to make out with any certainty where the middle of the opening lay. He could only steer blindly on and hope that he did not run the boat aground on one side or the other. That he made it to the open sea was more by luck than judgement; but having done so, he was unable to relax, for here the waters were in a turmoil and *Lucky Boy* was thrown about as if it had become a weightless thing and the gold inside it were no more burden than a bag of feathers.

He wished now that Jo and her friends had never come to him with that bar of gold. For that was when it had all started. And even then, if he and Blok had been content just to buy the stuff at a truly bargain basement price, all would have been well. They had been too greedy, that was the truth of it. And now it had come to this.

But they still might pull through. All was not yet lost. The cruiser was a fine craft and built for sea-going, built to face storms, though perhaps not one as severe as this. This was something unique in his experience. On his fishing trips with Blok the sea had usually been calm, the winds light. He had enjoyed taking the wheel then, felt himself no end of great guy, up there with the master mariners of the past – Columbus, Drake, Magellan and the solo voyagers like Slocum and Voss. What a conceited idiot he had been! Now he was faced with a real test of nerve and skill, and he knew how unfitted he was to handle this emergency that had been forced upon him.

Well, he had got the boat away from the island, and that was a start. The thing now was to keep her head to the wind and wait for the storm to pass. But how long would that be? Who could tell? And whatever happened, it was essential that the engine should not fail.

As soon as this thought came into his head it took root there and would not leave him. It nagged away at him, and he listened anxiously for any false note in the beat of the diesel, any signal that all might not be well in the heart of that indispensable piece of machinery.

When it did in fact fail he gave a cry as if of pain. And he blamed himself: if he had not thought about it perhaps it would not have happened. He had brought about the very event he had dreaded. He knew that this was mere superstition, but it stuck in his mind.

All his efforts to get the engine restarted were in vain, and now the cruiser was at the mercy of wind and wave. It was being blown helplessly along and was shipping water. He abandoned the attempt to get the engine going and left the wheelhouse in the possession of the corpse and made his way into the saloon.

There Jake and Wolf were still watching over Blok, who was breathing stertorously, the blood congealed on his face and forehead. Jake looked at him but said nothing.

'Engine's buggered,' Carlson said. 'Nothing we can do now, unless you feel like praying.'

He got no answer from the hunchback. Jake did not appear to be frightened; his face wore the same gloomy expression as ever. There was a dreadful racket going on in the saloon as the cruiser was tossed about by the waves, and the wind was shrieking like some weird creature trying to break in. At the far end of the saloon the pile of boxes containing the gold seemed to mock him. They were all his now. Jake had never been in on the deal, and maybe had no desire to be. And Blok looked like a goner, whatever happened. Seemed like the kraut in the wheelhouse was the first claimant, but he was dead too and probably had no genuine claim to the stuff either. Might have been difficult to find out who it did genuinely belong to now. But it made no difference: they were never going to get it.

He said: 'I was an idiot to come on this errand. Chances are the fat guy would have cheated me anyway. I had a nice little business back there. I should've been content. How about you, Jake? What are you thinking? Hell, man! Why don't you say something?'

'You talk too much,' Jake said.

It was some time later when the end came. There was an almighty shock and a sound of things breaking, cracking up. A shudder ran through the boat, and they were thrown around and some of the boxes tumbled off the pile.

'This is it,' Carlson said. And strangely, now that it had come, he no longer felt scared. It was as if all his fear had been used up and there was no more to be had. He was like a man who has stopped running because more running is useless. 'Now, Jake, we're for the high jump.'

And then the water came gushing in, and he knew that he was right.

27

Maybe

WHEN the yacht, *Wanderer*, sailed into the bay it was again doing its impersonation of a millpond on a still day. They dropped anchor and looked towards the shore and saw the wreckage of another yacht lying halfway up the beach on its side.

'Somebody's been here,' Laurie said.

The wreckage was a stark reminder of what might have been their own fate. But *Wanderer* had come through the storm with relatively little damage. The fact was that they had only been on the fringe of the hurricane and had escaped the worst of it. After it had passed on they had continued their voyage.

'That's true,' Rayburn said. 'And they didn't have much luck by the look of things.'

Jo was silent, frowning a little, as if the sight of the wreck had put some rather worrying thoughts into her head. She could have been trying to solve a puzzle, and not succeeding.

Pippa said: 'I wonder who they can have been. There's no sign of life. I guess we may find something when we go ashore.'

They did that without delay, eager to discover what they could. The wreck was on the right of where they beached the dinghy, and they walked over and examined it. There had been a lot of damage to the superstructure and both masts were broken, but the hull did not appear to have taken much punishment.

Laurie remarked that it looked as if it had been a pretty fine yacht, and Rayburn agreed.

'Got caught at anchor when the storm hit the island, I'd guess.'

'And the crew?' Laurie said.

'Ah, that's the question.'

There was no sign of anyone still alive, but there were footprints in the sand, some leading towards the trees. They followed the trail and came upon a body lying in the shade. Their first thought was that it was a corpse, but closer examination revealed that it was a sleeping man.

Laurie stirred him with his foot, and he woke and gazed up at them. He was wearing nothing but a pair of shorts, and he had fair hair and stubble on cheeks and chin.

'Are you okay?' Rayburn asked.

The man sat up. 'Yes,' he said, 'I am okay. And I am very glad to see you. I thought perhaps nobody would come – ever. And that would not be nice.'

'Looks like you had some trouble,' Rayburn said. 'That is your yacht back there?'

The man got to his feet. 'Yes, it is mine. The storm, you know. We were at anchor and got caught.'

'We? There were others?'

'Two. They are dead. I am the lucky one.'

'Who are you?' Rayburn asked.

'Sven Andersen, Danish. My companions were Heinz Müller and Otto Weyland. They were Germans.'

'But why did you come here?'

'We came to get the gold,' Andersen said.

They all stared at him.

'The gold!' Rayburn said. 'But how did you know it was here?'

'We knew because Müller was one of the men who buried it. They came in a U-boat. Later the U-boat was sunk and Müller was the only survivor. He waited a long time to return and claim the treasure; and now I do not know what has happened to him.'

'And the gold. Did you dig it up?'

'Oh, yes. We loaded it into the yacht.'

'So it's there now?'

'No.'

'Why not? What happened to it?'

'Come,' Andersen said. 'I will show you something.'

He started walking towards the rocks on the north shore, some two hundred yards away. The others followed. They came to the first of the rocks, and Andersen said:

'It is behind here. Follow me.'

He led them round the base of the rock and they saw that behind it, lying on the sand between it and the tidemark was the body of a man, almost naked; a large fat man with a battered face. Standing guard over the body was an Alsatian dog which bared its teeth and gave a low growl as they approached.

They did not need to be told who the dead man was. Even with the mutilation and the corruption of the flesh that had set in, they were certain of the identity.

'Blok,' Rayburn said.

'Ah!' Andersen said. 'So you know him.'

'Yes, we know him. But how did he get here? And the dog.'

'The dog has been my problem. It will not let me go near the body. I would have buried it otherwise – with the others.'

'Others?'

'Otto Weyland and the man whose name I do not know. I have brought food and water from my yacht for the animal, but still it does not trust me. But let us go away from here. It is not a pretty sight.'

They moved away and Andersen pointed to the yacht anchored in the bay.

'That is a much more pleasant sight to a man who has found himself marooned on a desert island. It is worth all the treasure in the world. But tell me now, who are you?'

Rayburn made the introductions, and Andersen acknowledged each with a nod of the head. Then he said:

'I am still puzzled. Why are you here?'

'We also came for the gold,' Rayburn said.

'So you knew about it. How was that?'

'We stumbled on it quite by accident not long ago. We took one of the gold bars as a sample. Blok was the man who bought it. He was going to buy the rest when we brought it.'

Andersen slapped his thigh. 'And then he double-crossed you. Thought he'd take the lot for himself before you could get your hands on it. Crafty man, that Blok.'

'But how did he get here?'

'In a big motor cruiser. We'd loaded the gold the previous day and were below decks when he came into the bay and latched on to us. The storm was brewing, and he came aboard uninvited with the other two and forced us to hand it over at gun-point. By the time the transfer had been made the storm was getting really bad, but somehow he managed to get out of the bay and we lost sight of the boat. It was only then we realized Müller was missing, and we guessed he must have stayed on board the cruiser.

'We were in trouble ourselves then, because the storm was still getting worse and the anchor would not hold. So what with the waves and the wind, we were thrown up on to the beach and smashed about like you see. Otto got a knock on the head, and it finished him. But I was lucky enough to escape with only a few bruises. Then when things eventually calmed down I took a look around and found the bodies washed up by those rocks. And I knew then that the cruiser didn't make it.'

He paused, rubbed the stubble on his chin, and added: 'I can tell you why. See that reef over there?' He pointed to the north, where a white line of foam could be seen where the coral just broke the surface. 'My guess is the cruiser was driven on to the reef and broke up. The dog must've swum ashore and the bodies were washed up later.'

'Bodies!' Laurie said. 'How many?'

'Two. Blok and another man. Not Müller or the hunchback.'

'Jake?'

'That's what Blok called him. Don't think the other man's name was mentioned. Anyway, I buried him as well as Otto. The spade we brought to dig up the gold came in handy for a different job.'

Rayburn was looking thoughtful. 'There's a question comes to my mind. How did Blok know the gold was on this island? We didn't tell him. We didn't tell anybody.'

Jo seemed uncomfortable, but she said nothing.

'That other man,' Rayburn said. 'The one without a name. What did he look like?'

'Oh, black hair, lean, small moustache. Some people might have called him handsome, I imagine.'

'Sound like anyone we used to know?' Rayburn said. And his gaze came to rest on Jo.

Pippa and Laurie were staring at her too.

'Don't look at me,' she said. 'I didn't tell him.'

'Now I wonder,' Rayburn said, 'just why I find that so difficult to believe.'

'Well, it's the truth.'

'Bullshit!' Laurie said. 'Who else could it have been? Who was hobnobbing with the bastard all the time we were ashore?'

Jo answered sulkily: 'Well, okay. So it may have slipped out when I wasn't thinking. But how was I to know what he and the Dutchman would cook up?'

'Are you saying you didn't?' Pippa demanded.

'Of course I am. You've got to believe me. Would I let you down like that? You're my friends, aren't you?'

'Not any more. Not me for one. I think we should leave you here to rot.'

'You can't do that.' Jo sounded alarmed, as though she thought it a real possibility. 'It would be murder.'

'Yes, it would, wouldn't?' Pippa said. And she turned her back on Jo.

It was out of the question of course. Even Pippa admitted that. She had only been trying to scare Jo, and with some success. But there would be no renewing of the friendship between the girls. Jo's ostracism made for an uneasy voyage back to Longville, especially as there was now an extra passenger on board. They had to leave the dog. There was no way they could have got it on board even if they had wanted to. It would have bitten anyone who came close enough to it. The most they could do was to leave some food and water for it, and it stayed where it was, guarding the dead body. In the end it would die too.

Rayburn told the girls that when they had been taken back home, that would be the end of the voyaging.

'We shall have to return to England. We're nearly out of funds and we'll have to go job-hunting. If we'd had the gold it would have been different, but as it is we've got no choice.'

Pippa looked sad on hearing this, but Jo appeared indifferent. She was already an outsider and she had told Pippa that the sooner she was shot of the lot of them, the better she would like it. Pippa took some pleasure in reminding her that if she had not thrown in her lot with that skunk Carlson she might now have been rich. Jo looked sour. She needed no reminding. This reflection plagued her constantly.

They were stopped by the Coast Guard cutter again when close to Longville: same boat, same two men boarding them in a search for contraband. As before, they found none.

'That paperweight,' Craig said. 'The one looked like a gold brick. Where is it?'

'We lost it,' Rayburn said.

'That was careless. Good thing it wasn't really gold.'

'Yes, it was, wasn't it?'

'Some guys are just plumb careless.'

'That's true as well,' Rayburn said. 'They let gold slip through their fingers like water.'

'Well, have a nice day,' Craig said.

Rayburn seemed to recall that he had heard that one before.

'You too,' he said.

Jo left with her kit as soon as they touched the jetty. Pippa hung around as though reluctant to leave. Andersen was staying with them. They had offered to take him with them, even across to Denmark. It would be their final voyage. He accepted the offer gratefully.

Pippa was still hanging around when evening came. Rayburn found her sitting on a bollard on the jetty.

'No home to go to?' he said.

'Guess not.'

'No more shacking up with Jo?'

'Never again. Not after what she did. It was mean; real mean.'

'And lost you your share of the gold.'

'Oh,' she said, 'I wasn't thinking about that. I'm not too bothered. Easy come, easy go. No, it was the treachery; that's what really got me. I wouldn't have believed she'd do a thing like that.'

They were both silent for a while, perhaps reflecting on that trachery, that meanness.

Then Rayburn said: 'If a man who had just lost out on the chance of a fortune; a man who had no job and no future worth speaking about, asked you to marry him, what would you say?'

'Well,' she said softly, 'it would depend on who the man was, wouldn't it?'

'Well, let's say for argument's sake the man's name was Stephen Rayburn, what then?'

'I'd say yes please.'

'You must be crazy,' Rayburn said.

'Well,' she said, 'that makes two of us, doesn't it?'

'My father is not going to be very pleased when he learns I've lost the yacht and there's no gold,' Andersen said.

They were in the Atlantic and making good progress towards home. But they were empty-handed.

'I suppose the yacht was insured,' Rayburn said.

'But not the gold.'

'No, not the gold.'

After a time Rayburn said: 'Maybe we could get some diving gear and go back and pick it up. It'll still be on the reef.'

'Maybe we could at that,' Laurie said.

They thought about it for a while, and then Rayburn said: 'On the other hand, maybe it would be best left where it is. It never did anybody any good. A lot of people lost their lives because of it.'

'That's true,' Andersen said. And then, after another period of silence, Rayburn said: 'On the other hand again, maybe it would be a pity just to leave it there. Maybe if it was put to a good use—'

'We could put it to a good use,' Laurie said.

'A very good use,' Pippa said.

'So maybe—'

Maybe.